"I'm not going to let anything happen to any of you, Maddie."

Kurt lowered his head. His next move was as instinctive as it was inevitable. He had wanted to kiss her for days, but this time he intended the kiss to be light, gentle. A tender gesture meant to soothe her fears and give her the assurance of his protection. But the instant he felt the softness of her lips, the taste of her, he wanted so much more. With all the willpower he could muster, he broke the kiss.

Her surprise was as evident as his own as she stared up at him.

For ten years she'd nourished her memory of the father of her son with fanciful yearnings and wishful dreams. Now, under the pressure of his lips, the warmth and power of his embrace, divine sensation spiraled to the pit of her stomach in a degree of aroused passion she had never suspected existed within her.

"Maddie, I want to make love to you."

Dear Reader,

It's been business as usual for the men of the Dwarf Squad, so Kurt Bolen (Code name: Sneezy), on medical leave due to a wound he received on the last mission, decides to make a quick visit to the small Wisconsin town in which he was raised. He is unprepared not only for the greatest and most unexpected surprise of his life, but also to find himself involved with illegal organ harvesters who are out to harm him and those near and dear to him.

I have to admit I've grown very attached to these guys in RATCOM, the CIA's Rescue and Anti-Terrorist Special Ops Squad, and the great gals they ended up marrying. If you liked Ann Bishop and Trish Cassidy, I'm sure you'll find Maddie Bennett just as appealing. Her mundane daily routine of running her bookstore takes on a whole new perspective when Kurt Bolen comes back to town.

I want to take this opportunity to thank you for the thoughtful cards and letters so many of you have sent Don and me during this chapter in our lives. Nothing is more rewarding than knowing there are unknown faces out there offering their prayers and support.

With Valentine's Day upon us, give that special person in your life a hug and kiss from me. And above all, have a happy and healthy winter.

My deepest love and affection,

Ana Leigh

ANA LEIGH

Heart at Risk

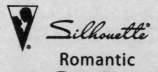

Romantic
SUSPENSE

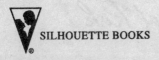

SILHOUETTE BOOKS

Recycling programs
for this product may
not exist in your area.

ISBN-13: 978-0-373-27620-2
ISBN-10:   0-373-27620-6

HEART AT RISK

Visit Silhouette Books at www.eHarlequin.com

Printed in U.S.A.

Books by Ana Leigh

Silhouette Romantic Suspense

ANA LEIGH

is a Wisconsin native with three children and five grandchildren. From the time of the publication of her first novel in 1981, Ana successfully juggled her time between her chosen career and her hobby of writing, until she officially retired in September of 1994 to devote more time to her "hobby." In the past she has been a theater cashier (who married the boss), the head of an accounting department, a corporate officer, and the only female on the Board of Directors of an engineering firm.

This *New York Times* and *USA TODAY* bestselling author received a *Romantic Times BOOKreviews* Career Achievement Award nomination for Storyteller of the Year in 1991, the Bookrak 1995-1996 Best Selling Author Award, the *Romantic Times BOOKreviews* 1995-1996 Career Achievement Award, and the *Romantic Times BOOKreviews* 1996-1997 Career Achievement Award for Historical Storyteller of the Year. Her novels have been distributed worldwide, including Africa, China and Russia.

I dedicate this novel to Kurt Kelley, a family friend
who is as dear to my heart as a son, and
who kept asking, "How's the book coming?"
Hey, here it is, Kurt!

Prologue

Colombia

The stillness was eerie. Black…noiseless…encompassing. No sound of distant voices, chirp of a cricket, chatter of a bird. Not a leaf stirred, nor a creature scurried as the six men hastened through the trees, their footsteps swathed in darkness and silence.

Suddenly the blackness was breached by a dim light filtered through the shutters of a window on the upper floor of a two-story stone building that stood like a monolith amid the scattered wooden shacks that surrounded it.

They had reached their target.

They'd been told that the local residents rarely ventured out at night, and despite the heat, kept their doors locked and shutters closed. Kurt could only hope tonight was no exception.

The strident bark of a dog split the stillness. Cassidy raised his hand, halting the squad. The barking ceased as quickly as it had begun and was too distant for their presence to have alerted the animal, so they moved on.

As they neared their objective, the squad pulled on their thermo night-vision goggles, casting the darkness into a sur-realistic green that enabled them to read the H sign hung above the front entrance of the building. To Kurt, a hospital meant sanctuary, a place of healing.

So how come I have a knot in my gut and goose bumps on my arms?

A door slammed and the men froze. The faint glow of a cigarette indicated the presence of a man, an automatic weapon hung from a strap on his shoulder.

"Make him?" Cassidy whispered. Kurt nodded. "Take him out."

Kurt raised the scoped sniper rifle and lined up the target. As soon as they heard the faint pop of the silencer, the squad moved quickly and entered the building.

Despite the wooden floor, the six men stole up the stairway without a sound and proceeded toward a lit room at the end of the hallway, halting to make sure each room they passed was deserted.

The final room had double doors that swung inward. Cassidy shoved up his goggles. The rest of the team did likewise, then waited as he peered cautiously through the glass in one of the doors. The wait seemed endless. He glanced at Don Larson beside him. Larson nodded, and tight-ened his hold on the weapon he carried. Cassidy and Larson would be the first two through the doors. The whole squad was tensed and wired. Ready to go. It was always like this right before the action.

Cassidy turned his head and mouthed the word *eight,* in-dicating there were eight armed men inside. The squad was outnumbered, but had the element of surprise—if not, all hell would have broken out by now.

He mouthed the word *nine* and made a slashing motion across his right arm to indicate there were nine unarmed people on the right side of the room.

They most likely were the six American hostages the squad had come to rescue, and probably three local medical people. Kurt could only hope that none of them would get hit when the gunfire started.

Cassidy stepped back, nodded then pushed open the doors.

Within seconds the shooting, shouting and cries of alarm had ended, and the fight was over. None of the team or hostages had been wounded and as the squad checked the bodies on the floor Cassidy announced, "Ladies and gentlemen, we're here to get you out. Please do exactly as told." He repeated the same message in Spanish.

A slim, middle-aged man stepped forward. "I am Dr. Fernando Escobar, head of this hospital," he said in accented but proper English. "We are grateful to you and your men, but I must offer medical assistance to any of those wounded men who require it."

Kurt shook his head when Cassidy glanced at him.

"None require it," Cassidy said succinctly.

"Then I must check my patients." The doctor went over to two hospital beds that had been shoved against a wall in the corner of the room. One of the women, obviously a nurse, joined him.

Cassidy turned back to the hostages. "Who's in charge among you?"

"I'm Dr. Eric Danvers," one of the men said. "We're a volunteer medical group. We come down here for a month each year to offer medical assistance."

"I'm aware of that, sir. And we're here to take you home.

Dr. Escobar, what about your staff and patients? Do you wish to be evacuated?"

"No, these patients are local villagers, the victims of for-profiting organ harvesting," Dr. Escobar replied. "It is a very common practice among the poor in this area. The harvesters come into a village, pay the locals a meager amount of money, extract the organs in a makeshift operating room and then dump the victims on our doorstep, not really caring if they live or die. None of us are in danger now. The terrorists were after the Americans."

"As you wish, sir," Cassidy said. "Did any of these men mention what terrorist group they belonged to?"

"No," Escobar replied. "But I am sure you know or you wouldn't be here." He turned back to his patients.

Kurt felt relieved when he heard the sudden tell-tale whir of a helicopter; their taxi had arrived—and punctual as usual.

With a wordless command Cassidy nodded to Rick Williams and Pete Bledsoe. They knew what was expected of them and led out.

Once they were airborne, the rescued hostages settled down and talked in low tones among themselves.

Too tired to follow the conversation, Kurt leaned his head against the wall, closed his eyes and thought about the mission.

Once again the Dwarf Squad had made it through without anyone seriously wounded. He couldn't help grinning when he thought how the Agency had tagged them the Dwarf Squad because they used the names of the seven dwarfs as code names. Then the grin slowly faded as he thought of Danny Sardino, code name Bashful, who had been killed in Beirut two years earlier. Danny had been the only squad member killed from the time they were formed.

These men were his brothers. His only family. Most had been SEALs when the CIA recruited them for RATCOM, the Agency's Rescue and Antiterrorist command. Rick Williams and Pete Bledsoe were the only exceptions—the two Brits had served in England's SAS. They'd been together for almost four years now. With the exception of Justin Anderson, who'd become a member of the squad six months before when Mike Bishop, the leader of the squad, had been pulled out and made deputy secretary of RATCOM. Dave Cassidy had moved up to squad leader.

And each man in the squad had an individual specialty—his was sharpshooter.

Together the six men were not only a family—they were a definitive weapon.

Chapter 1

Why in hell did I come back here? Kurt thought with disgust. I hated this damn town when I lived here.

In ten years the town hadn't changed much—still only one main street with one stoplight and one service station. The steeple of the Catholic church was still the tallest structure in town, and the courthouse with its portico and creaking rocking chairs looked like it could use a coat of fresh paint.

Kurt glanced at the grain store as he drove past it. The sign now read Cletis Tyler, Owner. So old man Tyler must have either died or retired, and his piss-ass son—and fellow class-mate—had taken over.

Jake's Tap was still the only tavern in town, the Dew Drop Inn the only motel. The post office was in the same spot, and the bank had a new brick facade. From what he could see, the only thing new was a two-story department store in the strip mall, boasting everything from safety pins to television sets. A woman's beauty salon called Curl Up with Shirley was a new addition also, and a pharmacy now occupied the space where Elsa's Bakery had been.

He used to love going to that bakery when he was a kid. It always smelled of freshly baked bread. Elsa Guttman, the kind old lady who owned it, would always slip him a sugar cookie. Maybe he had a few good memories of the town after all.

He was surprised at the sight of a tearoom and bookstore standing next to the old Rivoli Theatre. Now closed and boarded up, the letters on the theatre's once brightly lit canopy spelled out Building for Sale or Lease.

The balcony of the old theatre offered some fond teenage memories for Kurt as well...

If he kept it up, pretty soon he'd be blowing his nose and wiping the tears out of his eyes.

Yeah, right!

Kurt parked in front of Rosie's Diner. Twenty-five years ago Rosie Callahan had been the town hooker and earned her money the hard way—on her back. Much to the chagrin of half the guys in town, five years later she'd saved up enough money to open the only diner in town. By the time Kurt left town Rosie had just been elected mayor and was back to her old tricks in order to pay off campaign promises.

He popped seventy-five cents into a newspaper box and grabbed the *Vandergriff Sentinel*. A quick glance revealed that Carson Meadows was still the editor in chief, reporter and chief cook and bottle washer for that matter. Nothing changed except the price. It had gone up twenty-five cents in the past ten years.

Upon entering the diner Kurt perused the place from habit—the same eight stools at the counter, two connecting rows of six booths each, and six tables in the front near the window. The only change in the place was the color of the walls, and a large poster of Brad Pitt with sword in hand now hung where an earlier one of John Wayne with rifle in hand had reigned for the eighteen years he'd lived in the town.

The changing of the guard.

The place smelled of boiled cabbage, so he didn't have to be a rocket scientist to figure out the daily special. Kurt had beaten the dinner rush by about a half hour and the place was almost empty except for a couple and their kids in one of the booths and an old guy sitting at the counter.

The blond waitress who'd been talking to the old man glanced up when he entered. He'd have recognized Gertie Karpinski anywhere. She may have lost her youthful teenage glow, but there was no mistaking "Bare It and Share It" Karpinski. While most girls carried around lipstick, Gertie carried condoms. And in their four years of high school Gertie had lived up to her motto and bedded every guy in the graduating class—even that uptight jerk Cletis Tyler.

He headed for a booth, and could feel Gertie's eyes on him as he walked over, sat down and reached for the menu.

Surprise! Corned beef and cabbage *was* the special.

Gertie sauntered over to the booth and put down a glass of ice water, then pulled a pad and pencil out of her pocket.

"So what's it gonna be, good looking?"

He closed the menu. "How're you doing, Gertie?"

She did a double take. "Kurt Bolen! I don't believe it! Where have you been for the past ten years? Hope it wasn't in the slammer."

"No. I've been seeing the world, compliments of the U.S. Navy." It was a half-truth. He didn't mention the CIA. That was one job you didn't advertise.

"You back to stay?"

"Just passing through. What have you been up to? I never figured you'd hang around Vandergriff after graduation."

"I've been married and divorced a couple times."

"What about children?"

"Hell, honey, you know I'm too smart to let that happen. Besides, I'd be the mother from hell. What about you? Don't see no ring on your finger."

"Same as you, Gertie. I tried marriage, but it didn't work out. Fortunately there were no kids to get hurt by it."

Gertie patted his hand. "Guess we're just not the marrying types. But you sure don't look any worse the wear for it. Matter of fact, you look *great*." She reached out and squeezed his bicep. "Wow! I don't remember all that muscle."

Same old Gertie. Totally shameless. But he couldn't help liking her. He always had. She had a good sense of humor, and in school she'd never put on airs or tried to be anything other than honest about herself.

"So what's it gonna be, honey?"

For an instant he weighed whether she meant sex or food. He settled for the safer choice.

"Burger with the works and some fries, Gertie."

"Same old Kurt. I see your taste in food hasn't changed." She giggled throatily and leaned over. Her uniform was cut low enough to whet his appetite. "What about women?"

This time her message came through loud and clear. If the cleavage was the appetizer, his groin had begun to ratchet up for the main course.

He dragged his gaze away from her breasts and looked up and grinned. "Women all taste good to me, Gertie."

By the time Kurt finished reading the newspaper his food arrived. His training kicked in and he automatically checked out whoever came in as the diner began to fill up.

He was finishing up the burger when a young woman entered. The male in him—more than the CIA agent—assessed her as she approached a booth by the window where an older woman and young boy were seated.

She sure was hot. Damn hot! Late twenties with a hundred fifteen or twenty pounds curved lusciously on about five feet

seven inches. Soft curls of auburn hair feathered her forehead
and nape. His mom used to call it a feather cut, but there was
probably some fancy French name for it now. Whatever—his
fingers itched to dig into it.

But what really grabbed his attention were her green eyes.
They were slightly slanted—that Ava Gardner look that turned
a man on with a single glance.

She looked vaguely familiar to him and he figured they'd
probably been schoolmates. But the only redhead he remembered from school was Joey Bennett's sister, Mandy or Mattie,
or something like that. And she'd been lanky, wore geeky
glasses, and had long kinky red hair.

"Hey, Maddie, you're not going to believe this," Gertie
yelled out to the new arrival. "Kurt Bolen's back in town."

The woman jerked her head around and looked at him.
Maddie Bennett. So she *was* Joey's sister. Boy, had she changed!

Those jade eyes were wide with shock and she was looking
at him as if she'd seen a ghost.

Kurt was too flabbergasted to speak. He smiled and waved.
Maddie nodded slightly and then turned her head away.

He ordered a slice of pie and coffee, and as he ate, he
couldn't keep his mind off Maddie Bennett. He'd never rally
paid too much attention to Joey's sister, but still he couldn't
believe the change in her. Some past memory flitted on the
edge of his brain, but he couldn't nail it. What in hell difference did it make? He was out of there.

Kurt polished off the rest of his coffee, threw some bills
on the table, and got up to leave. His curiosity got the better
of him and he stopped at her booth on his way out.

"How have you been, Maddie?"

"Fine," she said. Despite her attempt at casualness he could
tell she was uptight. "What about you?"

"No complaints. How's Joey? Is he still living in Vandergriff?"

"Joey's dead. He joined the marines after graduation and was killed in Afghanistan."

"I'm sorry to hear that. We had some good times together."

The older woman extended her hand. "I'm Elizabeth Bennett, Maddie's Aunt Beth. I don't believe we've met."

"Kurt Bolen," he said, shaking her hand.

Elizabeth Bennett smiled warmly. He was struck by the beauty of the gray-haired woman. Unlike her niece—who at the moment appeared to be so tense she looked ready to pop—Elizabeth Bennett had a serenity that enhanced her loveliness. But regardless, both women were knockouts. The family must have one hell of a gene pool!

"Kurt graduated with Joey and me, Aunt Beth," Maddie said.

Elizabeth Bennett frowned in concentration. "Bolen? Of course! Was your father Charles Bolen?"

"Yes he was. Did you know him?"

Here it comes: Kurt Bolen, the no good kid from Stoneville, whose father was the town drunk.

"I'm a retired nurse, Kurt. I was on duty the night they brought your father into the hospital," she said sadly. "Such a tragic accident."

Changing the subject quickly, she smiled and slipped her arm around the young boy's shoulders. "And this handsome lad is Maddie's son Scotty."

He reached out a hand. "Hi, pal."

The boy hesitated momentarily, as if he didn't know what to do. Then, as if pleased with the manly gesture, the boy grinned and shook his hand.

Kurt glanced at Maddie: Uptight and Gorgeous looked like she was holding her breath. And he discovered Elizabeth Bennett was studying him intently. What was with these two women? He had to fight the urge to reach down and check if his fly was open.

"After all these years what brought you back to Vandergriff, Kurt?" Elizabeth Bennett asked.

"Just passing through. I'm being treated at the Vet hospital in Milwaukee and I thought I'd drive out and see the old hometown."

"Oh, I hope it's not anything too serious." Elizabeth's concern seemed genuine.

"I blew a kneecap, but at least I'm off the crutches now."

Elizabeth's face creased with sympathy. "Oh my. I'm sorry to hear about that. It must be painful. So you're in Milwaukee, you say?"

"I expect to leave there tomorrow and go home."

"Where is your home?"

"In D.C." Kurt started to back away. "Well, I better get going. Nice meeting you, Ms. Bennett."

"Yes, and I hope your leg heals swiftly. Take care of yourself, dear boy."

"Thank you. Nice seeing you again, Maddie."

"Yes, take care of yourself," Maddie echoed.

Her face didn't crack a smile. Ava Gardner eyes or not, she was one edgy female. But come to think of it, she'd been that way ten years ago, too.

Since she wasn't wearing a wedding ring, she was either widowed or divorced, and he couldn't help wondering how long it'd been since she'd been laid. With her looks... *Oh, hell, grow up, Bolen!*

He winked at the boy and departed. Once he was in his car, Kurt realized he'd been so distracted by Maddie that he hadn't said goodbye to Gertie. Well, tomorrow morning he'd stop in for breakfast and say it then—for the sake of the good old times.

Elizabeth Bennett watched Kurt Bolen walk to his car. A slight limp was perceptible, but he appeared to be coping remarkably well with it. "My goodness, he certainly appears to be a fine young man, doesn't he?"

"He's okay," Maddie said.

Beth eyed her niece warily. "Just okay? Honey, you're too young for that kind of reaction. He's gorgeous."

"And you, Aunt Beth, are too old for yours."

"I liked him," Scotty declared.

"What was he like ten years ago?" Beth asked. "He's too good-looking for you not to have noticed."

"For goodness' sake, Aunt Beth, what difference does it make? He's been gone for ten years. We rarely spoke. I don't think he even remembered my name. He and Joey hung around together, so *that* was always trouble looking for a place to happen. Kurt left town right after graduation, and that's the last I saw or heard of him until a couple minutes ago."

Maddie reached across the table and squeezed Scotty's hand. "So have you decided what you're having to eat, sweetheart?"

"I'll have a hamburger and French fries."

"Scotty, that's all you ever order when we eat out."

"Hamburger and French fries are my favorite meal."

Maddie chuckled and tousled his thick growth of dark hair. "How will you ever know until you try something different?"

Beth only half listened to the exchange between mother and son as she watched Kurt pull away in a red Charger. Despite Maddie's attempt to be casual, Beth could see her niece was still very upset over this chance meeting with Kurt Bolen. This piqued her curiosity. Something here didn't quite add up…

Beth choked back a gasp when she suddenly realized what it might be, and her mouth curved in a pleased smile. *Yes, Kurt Bolen, take good care of yourself. I have great plans for you.*

Kurt pumped up the pillow for the dozenth time and leaned back on the bed. The old Laurel and Hardy movie ended and he grabbed the remote and started to channel hop. Television sucked. It bored him royally unless it was a football or basketball game.

Besides, in the six months since his injury, he'd watched enough television to last him a lifetime. He loathed sitcoms, they were an unrealistic picture of family life—at least the family life he remembered. The multitude of crime and horror shows did nothing but demonstrate ghoulish ways to torture and murder. And as for all the alien and paranormal characters, there was no worse monster on this earth than a terrorist with an UZI or a Rocket Propelled Grenade launcher in his hands.

Kurt turned off the tube and tossed aside the remote in disgust. He got out of bed and walked to the window. It was Saturday night and only a little past nine o'clock; the town had rolled up its streets already. Hot time in the old town tonight!

Well he was too edgy to stay cooped up in the motel room. He pulled on his jeans, shirt and shoes and went out. He should have taken up Gertie's offer at the diner. Instead he'd gotten diverted by Maddie Bennett. Boy that woman was hot! But why in hell did she disturb him so much? There was something about her he couldn't remember, but it would come to him.

Without any destination in mind, he ended up on Poorman's Peak, the bluff that overlooked Stoneville's shanties and railroad tracks where he'd grown up. Kurt parked, then sat gazing down on the site. Light glowed from the factory that sprawled several blocks in length. The second shift was hard at work.

He'd been raised on the "wrong side of the tracks" in the part of town disparagingly called *Stoneville,* because of the quarry that furnished the major employment for Stoneville's residents. He'd had no siblings and had run with a tough group of boys. His folks had worked in the quarry and one night in Kurt's freshman year of high school, his drunk father had staggered in front of a moving train. Two years later his mother had died of lung cancer.

He'd toughed it out alone and finished school. The morning following graduation he'd gone to Milwaukee and enlisted in the navy, got married three years later and six months after that went through a bitter divorce.

The United States Navy had been his salvation. It had steered him on a course away from the gutter he'd been heading into and toward becoming a Navy SEAL and ultimately a member of the CIA's Dwarf Squad. It had given him the close brotherhood and inviolable friendships of the other squad members. Now faced with the possibility that the squad would be disbanded, he feared the loss of a family again.

There was no kidding himself. That was the real reason for his irritability, his impatience and disgust with everything that crossed his path. The writing was on the wall. Sure as hell RATCOM was going to be disbanded. His family was going to be busted up.

Kurt sighed and looked down on Stoneville. Yeah, for damn sure there wasn't anything sentimental about this "sentimental journey" home. First thing in the morning he'd climb into his car and Vandergriff, Wisconsin, would see the last of him. This time for good.

Just as he turned the ignition key to leave a car drove up and parked a short distance away.

As he backed out, the headlights of his car revealed the driver of the other car. He recognized Maddie Bennett at once. What in hell was she doing up here alone? Waiting for some guy, no doubt. And he was probably married. Why else would they meet up here unless they didn't want anyone in town to see them?

Well, uptight or not, it figured if she wasn't still married there'd be some guy banging her. The thought disappointed him. Why did a gal with an angel face and Ava Gardner eyes have to settle for making out with a married man in the seat of a car?

Suck it up, Bolen. Not your problem. Your problem is that you're not the guy she's waiting for.

Chapter 2

Maddie's brief encounter with Kurt Bolen had resurrected memories best forgotten, and she'd been in a near panic ever since. Ten years had only enhanced his dark-haired, brown-eyed handsomeness. She'd had a crush on him from the time she'd first seen him when the Bennetts had moved to Vandergriff her final year of high school.

Recalling those long-ago days was painful to her now—almost as painful as they'd been then. Since her father worked for the quarry company, they, too, were one of the "Stoners" that the town looked down upon.

It's ancient history, Maddie, so why dredge it up?

She didn't have to ask herself that; she knew the answer. How often in the past ten years had she driven up here to Poorman's Peak and recalled the last time she had seen Kurt Bolen—the night of their high school graduation? And now tonight, she'd turned her head and there he was.

She'd had no close friends that last year of high school and spent most of her time alone, so why she'd even gone to the graduation party at Gertie Karpinski's was still a mystery to her. After she'd sat in a corner being ignored for two hours, she had decided to leave. On the way out she'd encountered Kurt Bolen sitting on the steps outside.

Kurt and Joey were part of the same gang, but Kurt had never paid any attention to his friend's shy, freckle-faced sister. Why should he? Every gal in the school had the hots for him.

Throughout the evening she'd stolen peeks at him. He'd spent most of his time sneaking drinks from the flask in his pocket and was too drunk to even remember her name. As if he'd ever remembered her name.

She had declined his offer of a drink, but had gotten up the nerve to sit down and talk to him. It was the first time they'd been alone—and he'd actually spoken more to her than "Hi."

When she'd stood up to leave, Kurt had offered to drive her home. Even though he'd been inebriated, she'd accepted. On the way home he'd driven up to Poorman's Peak and parked. Since it was still early and the party was still going strong, they'd been the only car.

But kids didn't come there for the view; they came to make out. In his drunken state Kurt had leaned over and kissed her—and then kissed her again. She could still remember the smell of the whiskey on his breath, and even more intoxicating, the excitement of his nearness and thrill of his kisses. Having worshipped him from afar she'd been too enthralled to resist when he'd slipped the dress off her shoulders and made love to her. It had been the most divine memory of her life, and despite the hardships that followed, she'd never ceased to cherish those stolen moments. He had fallen asleep—or more likely passed out. She'd driven him home, parked the car in front of the shack where he lived and left him undisturbed.

The next morning she'd overheard Joey telling their mother

Kurt had left town. A couple of months later she was certain she was pregnant.

Determined to raise the child, she'd refused to reveal the father's name and ignored her parents' suggestion to abort the pregnancy or put the baby up for adoption.

Her brother Joey had gone off and enlisted in the marines and shortly before Scotty was born, her parents were shot to death when the bar they were in had been held up. Aunt Beth had taken her in and helped her to raise Scotty.

With Beth's help Maddie had been able to go to a junior college in the morning and work the second shift at the quarry. After earning an associate's degree, and with her aunt as a cosigner, Maddie had been able to borrow enough from the bank to open a bookstore and tiny tea shop. It had been ten years of constant struggle and hard work, but at least her son would not end up as a Stoner.

And now Kurt Bolen had appeared from nowhere. She harbored no bitterness toward him. How could she, when he was responsible for giving her the most precious thing in her life— her son. But she also realized he could threaten everything.

Was it fair not to tell Kurt the truth about Scotty? Was she being selfish, and not considering what would be best for her son?

Obviously Kurt had no intention of remaining in Vandergriff, but what if he demanded equal parental rights? She knew nothing about him or what he'd been doing for the past ten years. He'd been pretty wild when he was younger. She couldn't imagine turning Scotty over to this stranger on alternate weekends and such. And that could very well happen if Kurt demanded it.

And what if he was abusive or a drunkard? He'd always drank heavily, even on the night Scotty was conceived. To reveal the truth to him now would only open a can of worms that could have a negative effect on Scotty's life and her own.

No matter how much she'd held on to those girlish fantasies through the years of Kurt coming back to town for her, she was no longer an irresponsible teenager. Her responsibility—and only consideration—was for the welfare of her son.

She would not let anything or anyone threaten that welfare.

After checking out of the motel the next morning, Kurt filled the gas tank, went to the diner and ate breakfast then said goodbye to Gertie.

Once outside he took a final look around, climbed into his car and turned on the ignition. "Goodbye forever, Vandergriff."

Last night had resurrected too many memories. He wanted to get back to Milwaukee then home to D.C.

He took a shortcut on a back road to get to the I-94 Expressway. Nearing an old abandoned quarry that had filled with water during the years, he thought of the many times he'd used it as a swimming hole when he was a kid.

He slowed his speed when he saw a young boy skimming stones into the water. As he got closer, he recognized Scotty Bennett, and saw that Elizabeth Bennett, wearing a floppy, wide-brimmed hat to shade her face and eyes from the hot sun sat on a rock nearby. Times sure had changed since he was a kid. Back then, no one thought you needed a babysitter when you were a nine-year-old playing outside.

Kurt tooted the car horn and waved. Scotty spun around, recognized Kurt, and attempted to wave back. He lost his balance, staggered backward and toppled into the water.

Kurt slammed down on the accelerator and sped to as near the edge of the quarry as he could get. Elizabeth had just reached it.

"Can he swim?" he shouted to her, dashing out of the car.

"Not very well," she said. "Oh, dear God!"

Peering down into the hole, Kurt saw the struggling boy

surface then go under again. He pulled off his shoes and dove in, then felt a shock of pain to his knee when he hit the water.

Visibility was poor in the murky water and without goggles it was difficult to see. After several painful dives, he caught sight of Scotty and brought him to the surface.

Elizabeth was on her cell phone calling 911 for help and came quickly to his aid to help get Scotty out of the water. Kurt's knee was throbbing and by the time he succeeded in hoisting himself out, Elizabeth had Scotty stretched out on his back and was attempting to give him CPR to get some air into the unconscious boy's lungs.

Kurt took over the rhythmic procedure and after several more attempts Scotty began to spit up water. Kurt quickly flipped him onto his side as the boy regurgitated the water out of his lungs. "Elizabeth, get the blanket from the backseat of my car."

She nodded and hurried to get it. By the time the volunteer fire department and every other emergency vehicle in town arrived with sirens blazing and lights flashing, Scotty was wrapped snugly in a blanket and sitting up coughing a bit but coherent.

The paramedic with the fire department checked Scotty's vital signs. Satisfied, he packed up his emergency equipment. "He'll be fine. His lungs sound clear and the rest of his vital signs are okay, Ms. Bennett."

Beth had remained calm and efficient throughout the whole ordeal. "Thank you, Kevin. How's the new baby doing?"

"Mother and child doing fine," he said. "And Sandy loves the sweater and booties you knit for the baby." He shook his head. "Each summer we have to pull a kid out of that hole. The county should either drain it and fill it with dirt and rocks, or build a fence around it. Last year one of the kids wasn't as lucky as Scotty here. We lost him."

When the vehicles had all departed Elizabeth grasped Kurt's hand. That steel control she'd maintained throughout the ordeal had dissipated, and her voice trembled when she tried to speak.

"How can I ever thank you enough, Kurt. Scotty would have drowned if you…" The bubble finally burst. She couldn't go on, and broke down sobbing.

Kurt put his arms around her and let her cry. It would do her good.

"I'm sorry," Scotty said sorrowfully, tears streaking his cheeks. "I feel real bad that I made you cry. Please don't cry anymore, Aunt Beth."

Elizabeth knelt beside the boy and kissed him, then dried her tears and held him in the circle of her arms.

"Sweetheart, it wasn't your fault. I'm just so happy you're okay. I think I better get you home and into some dry clothes."

Kurt started to hobble back to his car. He had some pain pills in his pack, but rarely used them to avoid becoming dependent on them. Right now the pain was too severe to try and tough it out.

"Oh, dear, you injured your leg again, didn't you?" Elizabeth asked.

"I'm sure it's nothing serious. I aggravated it when I dove into the water."

"Well I insist you come home with me and let me check it out. Besides, you're soaking wet and should change into dry clothing."

The last thing he wanted to do was go back into town. But he did want to get out of his wet clothes.

"I can change right here, Ms. Bennett."

The sweet old lady's countenance hardened into a stern frown. "I do not intend to stand here and argue with you, young man. You're coming home with me."

The issue was settled.

In a lighter vein she added, "Besides, you wouldn't abandon us out here, would you?"

"How did you get here?"

"We walked. Are you able to drive, or should I?"

"My right leg's fine, Ms. Bennett."

"And please drop the formality," she declared. "I'm either Beth or Aunt Beth. Whichever you prefer. And I think I should probably drive."

"Yes, ma'am," Kurt replied, tempted to snap off a salute.

"Come on, honey," she said to Scotty, slipping an arm around his shoulder and helping him into the car.

Once they were on their way, a twinkle appeared in Beth's eyes. "You take orders very well, Kurt."

"A habit I picked up in the military," he said.

"Army, navy or marines?"

"Navy."

"How long have you been in?" she asked.

"I enlisted right after graduation."

"What's your rank?"

"Actually, I'm not in the navy anymore."

Her surprise was apparent. "What do you do for a living?"

"I work for the government."

He was spared any more of the interrogation when she pulled into the driveway of a two-story, cream-colored house with black shutters and roof.

Scotty appeared none the worse for his near drowning. He jumped out of the car and raced ahead into the house.

Beth stayed behind to offer a helping hand to Kurt, who appeared to be the only casualty of the incident.

Beth insisted he shower to cleanse the quarry water off him. By the time he finished, the painkillers had kicked in and eased the pain considerably.

"Give me your wet clothing and I'll wash it with Scotty's."

"That's not necessary. I'll pack up and get out of here."

"I won't hear of it," Beth declared as she took the wet

clothes from him. "It won't take long and in the meantime I've made a fresh pot of coffee. So just sit down and relax."

She returned a few moments later, put a plate of chocolate chip cookies on the table and poured them each a cup of coffee.

Beware of maiden aunts bearing chocolate chip cookies. What was she up to?

Suddenly the door burst open and Maddie rushed in. Kurt doubted she even noticed his presence. "Where is he?" she asked breathlessly.

"Relax, dear. Scotty's taking a bath. Kevin gave him a clean bill of health."

Beth could have saved her breath. Maddie rushed past and up the stairs. She returned moments later.

"The bathroom door's locked and he won't open it. He said he prefers privacy when he bathes." Her mouth curved in the barest suggestion of a grin. "Privacy! I'm his mother! That little munchkin! I ought to warm his bottom when he comes out."

"I know, dear, I got the same response, and I'm a nurse. So sit down and have a cup of coffee with us."

For the first time since she arrived, Maddie looked directly at him. Kurt cut her some slack. Her concern for her son was understandable.

"Thank you, Kurt. Aunt Beth told me on the phone that you're responsible for saving Scotty."

"I just happened to be in the right place at the right time. Besides, if I hadn't waved at him, he probably wouldn't have fallen."

"If anyone's to blame, I am," Beth protested. "I never should have let him get that close to the rim of that hole."

Maddie took a deep draft of the coffee. "Please, neither of you are to blame. Accidents happen. I just thank God Scotty's okay."

"We all are, dear," Beth said. "Except for Kurt. He aggravated his knee injury when he jumped into the water."

Despite her anxiety for her son, Maddie looked contrite. "I'm sorry, Kurt."

"No sweat. It's happened before. I just have to take it easy for a while. I'll have the doc check it out when I get back to the VA hospital."

Beth handed him the plate of cookies. "It's a long drive back to Milwaukee. And you shouldn't drive after taking those pain pills. I think you should rest right here for a couple of days. There are twin beds in Scotty's room, so you can double up with him."

"It's only a couple hours' drive, Beth."

"And you only took a couple pills. I won't hear of it. We insist you remain right here." Beth looked at Maddie for support. "Don't we, dear?"

Aunt Beth was sniffing the wrong scent if she expected her niece to back her up. Maddie looked anything but supportive. "Well…ah…I understand why Kurt would want to get back to proper medical care."

"I beg your pardon, Missy," Beth declared, feigning indignation. "I happen to be a registered nurse."

"But you don't have X-ray eyes, do you, darling?" Maddie hurried from the room and went back upstairs.

They heard her pound on the bathroom door. "Scotty, you've been in that bath long enough. Unlock this door, or I'm getting the key and coming in."

"Okay, I'll be out in a minute," the boy yelled back. "Boy, a kid's got no privacy living in a house full of women."

"*Hasn't* any privacy," Maddie corrected. "Furthermore, you'll have even less if you're not out of there in the next sixty seconds."

"How can I have less of what I don't have to begin with?"

"You'll find out soon enough if you don't listen to me."

Beth smiled. "Hope you don't get the wrong impression, Kurt. Right now Maddie's aching so badly, she's about to burst if she can't get her arms around that boy and judge for herself that he's okay. They're very close and he's her whole life." She shook her head. "Lord, if anything would have happened to Scotty, Maddie would never have been able…"

Kurt reached over and patted her hand. "I understand. It's not hard to tell they're tight. What about his father? Is he alive, or is Maddie divorced?"

"Oh, he's very much alive."

"Where is he?"

"Right here in Vandergriff."

"Does he know about the accident?"

"Yes," she said. She looked up and smiled. "Scotty will be glad to hear that you're staying for a couple of days. Now there'll be another man in the house."

"Beth, I didn't say I was staying," he said.

"But you will, won't you, dear." She smiled confidently and picked up their cups and carried them to the sink.

In the past ten years he'd been his own man, made his own decisions unless the military made them for him. But no one talked him into doing anything he didn't want to do—and right now he wanted to get the hell out of there as quickly as he could.

With that firm resolution in mind he opened his mouth and said, "Okay, but just until tomorrow."

Kurt glanced at Maddie who had just come down the stairs. She didn't look happy—appalled would be more correct. He swung his gaze back to Beth. She looked like the cat who'd just swallowed the canary.

So why did he suddenly feel like he'd just stepped into a steaming pile of horse manure?

Chapter 3

"Boy, this is cool," Scotty said when Kurt brought his backpack into the bedroom. "I never had a roommate before."

"You mean you've never had a sleepover?"

"Oh, sure, but that's not the same as someone staying for more than one night. How long you gonna stay, Mr. Bolen?"

"Sorry, pal, just for tonight," Kurt said. Unless he could think of a good excuse for leaving right away.

"I cleaned out one of my dresser drawers. You can put your clothes in it, Mr. Bolen."

"That's not necessary, Scotty. I'll keep them in my pack. And just call me Kurt. I'm not used to such formality."

"My mom said it's not polite to address an elder person by their first name."

"Maybe a woman—but we fellows have to stick together, right?" He gave Scotty a high five and the boy grinned.

"Aunt Beth brought in some extra hangers so's you can hang up your shirts and pants."

"That was very nice of her, but I only have a couple shirts, and an extra pair of jeans. I didn't figure on staying away too long."

"You mean from the hospital in Milwaukee?" Compassion now glowed in the boy's blue eyes that only seconds before were alight with happiness. "Does your leg hurt real bad?"

"Naw...nothing to worry about. Tomorrow it'll be fine."

"I hope not." He blushed in embarrassment. "I mean, I hope you don't have any more pain, but I want you to stay longer."

As Kurt glanced around the room, a thought crossed his mind. "Do you have a computer, Scotty?"

"No, but my mom does down at the bookstore. Sometimes she brings it home with her. We could go down and get it."

"No, forget it. I just thought I'd pass some time chatting with a couple friends on the Internet."

"Sometimes when I'm at the bookstore Mom lets me play a game on the Internet, but that's all. She said there are naughty pictures and per..."

"Perverts," Kurt said.

Scotty nodded. "She said these perverts lurk on the Internet trying to se...ah..."

"Seduce?" Kurt asked.

"Yeah, that's the word. They hurt young kids." He frowned. "How can they do that, Kurt, if they don't even live here?"

This was as bad as trying to explain the birds and the bees to the kid. "They pretend to be your friend to find out where you live. If you're too young to come to them, they'll come to you."

"I guess I don't have to worry 'cause I don't have a computer. You can watch television if you like." He walked over and turned on a small set on the corner of a desk.

Kurt picked up the remote, sat down on the edge of the bed and began to channel surf. The choices were limited.

"My mom had a chip put on the channels I shouldn't watch."

"Can't get away with anything today, can you?"

He hit a news channel and was about to move on when the newscaster mentioned the world-wide spread of criminal organ harvesting. Recalling what he had observed while in Colombia, Kurt listened to the discussion between the panel of three men and a woman. He was surprised to see that one of the panelists was Dr. Escobar, the doctor in charge of the hospital in Colombia.

According to the panelists, organ donations were needed all over the world but the demand was so much greater than the supply that in many countries innocent victims were being attacked and would wake up missing vital organs.

"Kurt, what's organ harvesting?" Scotty asked.

Kurt switched off the tube. "Prior to dying, Scotty, many people indicate that they want their organs donated to others who are in need of them."

"Like what?" Scotty asked.

"There's a multitude of things, pal. Hearts, lungs, kidneys, livers. All sorts of things. Even skin."

"Wow! You mean you can take something from someone's body and put it in somebody else's?"

"Well, it's a pretty tricky procedure but yes, you can and it saves thousands of people's lives."

"Kids' lives, too."

"Sure. Babies born with damaged heart valves and things like that. It's amazing. Of course, there has to be a lot of things in play to make it successful. The donor would have to have been in good health—most likely died from an accident. Then the organ has to be removed when the donor is legally brain dead, but still has a functioning heart and lungs. In other words, the organs would be useless if removed after there ceased to be oxygen being transported to those areas."

Scotty frowned. "If a person's dead, how can that happen?"

"Machines, Scotty. A person's brain can be mush, but machines can keep them alive to remove these organs and such in time. And a person doesn't have to be dead to donate an organ. Many people legally donate organs to family members and others in need in order to save their lives. Kidneys and bone marrow are good examples of what a healthy person can donate without dying to do so."

"What about arms and legs. If a person was dying could you donate them, too?"

"I don't think so, Scotty. At least I've never heard of it. I've heard of reattaching fingers and hands, but they were the victim's to begin with."

"Maybe someday the doctors will figure out how to do that, too, then no one would have to use a wheelchair or a pro..."

"Prosthesis," Kurt said. He tousled the young boy's hair. "Yeah, maybe someday."

He liked this kid. He had never had much to do with children before, but it was almost as if he and Scotty had bonded on sight.

Unfortunately the same could not be said about him and Maddie. The woman seemed to dislike him on sight. So maybe he was a bit on the wild side when they were in school. How long can she carry a grudge? That was ten years ago— *so let it go, lady!*

Later Kurt sat down to have dinner with the Bennetts. He couldn't remember sitting down as a family with anyone since he was young. Sure he and the squad had eaten countless meals together, but this was the first time it was a regular family meal with women and a child. Mike and Dave had only gotten married within the last year, and the rest of the guys were single.

He had to say he enjoyed it. Homemade fried chicken, mashed potatoes and gravy, fresh Wisconsin corn on the cob. It all tasted different than in a restaurant. Either these two women were the best cooks in the world, or it just felt good to be a normal guy sitting around at a dinner table.

Besides, the company was great. Aunt Beth was a charming conversationalist, Maddie was quiet but good to look at, and the kid was a joy. It made Kurt begin to think about what he'd been missing all these years.

"Mom," Scotty suddenly asked, "if I would have died this morning, would you have donated my organs to kids who need them?"

The startling question clearly caught her off guard, and Maddie's fork clunked against the plate as it slipped through her fingers. "What?"

"I've decided that when I die I want my organs donated to help other kids who need them."

Still startled, Maddie asked, "Scotty, where did you get such an idea?"

"Kurt and I were watching the television and they were talking about it."

Oh, oh, Kurt thought, *hang on to your head, Bolen, I think the ax is about to fall.*

"Scotty, I've told you it's disrespectful for a child to address an adult by a first name."

Kurt came to the boy's defense. "It's my fault, Maddie, I told him he could."

She turned a disapproving gaze on him. "That may be so, Mr. Bolen, but my son knows *my* wishes on the subject."

"I personally have no objection to it."

"And I'm also very selective about Scotty's television viewing, Mr. Bolen."

For God's sake! The woman was chastising him as if he were a two-year-old. "It was a news channel, Maddie."

"Good gracious, Maddie, I'm sure no harm was done," Beth said. "And I think Scotty's consideration for those less fortunate is very admirable."

"That's not the point, Aunt Beth. It's a very unpleasant subject and I doubt Scotty understands it."

"I do, too," Scotty said. "Kurt explained it to me. Mom, do you know that in some countries there are bad guys who steal the organs from innocent people? And in China they remove organs from executed bad guys and then sell them."

Maddie paled, but forced a smile. "I think we should change the subject. And in the future, Scotty, if you have any questions about organs and such bring them to me and don't bother our guests with them."

"Yes, Mom," Scotty said, hanging his head.

Kurt was pissed. If Maddie was so hung up on what was proper and improper, why lecture the poor kid in front of a stranger, instead of waiting until she and Scotty were alone? But he bit his tongue to keep from saying what was on his mind. There was no sense in expressing his opinion to this uptight female. She only made him aware that he didn't really belong.

Which was true. So what in hell was he doing here anyway?

Kurt stood up. "Ladies, thank you for dinner. It was delicious, and I can't remember the last time I had a home-cooked meal. But I think it'll be best if I leave now."

"Oh, Kurt, I wish you would spend the night," Beth said. "You should rest that leg, and it's a long drive back to Milwaukee."

"I've imposed on your hospitality enough. Thank you for everything."

Scotty pushed back his chair and ran sobbing up the stairs.

Hell, now he would have to face the kid to get his pack out of the bedroom. What a mess!

"Would you care for coffee and dessert before you leave?" Beth asked.

"No, thank you. I think I should get going before it gets too late."

Beth got up and began to carry dishes into the kitchen.

"I'm sorry, Mr. Bolen," Maddie said.

"Feel free to call me Kurt. I think you're old enough."

"I guess I deserve that. Do you mind stepping outside? I'd like to talk to you for a few minutes."

They moved outside and sat down on a swing on the front porch. "I know you think I'm very rude, and I apologize," she said. "When I heard about Scotty's accident I fell apart, and however I may appear to you, I want you to know I'm deeply grateful. I shall always be."

This was worse than an award ceremony with some stuffy navy commander pinning a purple heart or silver star on him.

"Look, Maddie, it's over. Let it go. I did what any guy would have done."

"I don't want you to leave with the impression I'm ungrateful."

"Fine. I believe you. So I'll be going—"

"You think I'm wrong, don't you?" she suddenly blurted out.

"Chill out, lady. I'm leaving." His unexpected response caught her off guard and once again those green eyes widened with surprise.

"You don't understand," she said.

"You've got that right. You always this uptight?"

She drew a deep quivering breath as if it were her last one. "It's just that all this has been very upsetting to me."

"Well, like I said, it's over. Scotty's fine. So let it go. There'll be other things you'll have to deal with while he's growing up. You can't protect him from everything in life. There's no way you can keep him from stumbling and falling sometimes. Just hope it's not into another quarry," he said, in an attempt to lighten the conversation.

"So you don't agree with the way I'm raising Scotty."

"Doesn't matter what I think."

"Would you believe me if I told you it does."

"Frankly no, Maddie. So don't try to tell me you give a good goddamn what someone like me thinks."

She looked him straight in the eye. "You're wrong. You have no idea how wrong you are."

Kurt stood up to leave. "I'm not into this kind of scene, so I'll get my pack and get out of here."

"Kurt, you don't understand. I'm not trying to be sarcastic. Your opinion is important to me."

He looked at her a moment then flopped down again, jarring the swing. "Lady, you asked. In the short time I've been here, I have the impression you're an uptight female too set in your ways. You're smothering the kid. Once in a while it wouldn't hurt to let Scotty make some of his own choices. Chips on his television, so he won't watch what you don't want him to. Ever think of trusting the kid? Putting him on his honor? Let him make the choice of the path he'll take?"

"He's only nine years old. I don't believe he's old enough to make the right choices."

"You'll never know until you let him try."

She appeared to be struggling with her thoughts and he knew he had no right to express his opinions. But dammit, she had rubbed him wrong with her officious attitude at dinner.

"Maddie, I know I was pretty wild as a kid, so I'm a poor example to be giving lectures on child rearing, but maybe Scotty and I have the same problem. Neither of us had a father figure to emulate. My dad was the town drunk and I was embarrassed and ashamed of his actions. Scotty's being raised by two women in a manless household. He needs some positive masculine influence in his life the same way that I did. How much contact does he have with his father?"

"None."

"What? His dad lives right here in Vandergriff and Scotty has no contact with him! Is that your idea or his father's?"

"Who told you Scotty's father lives here?"

"Beth mentioned it earlier."

"Well, it's not true. Beth doesn't know who Scotty's father

is. Nobody does but me." She drew a deep breath. "I've never married nor told anyone the name of the man who fathered him."

You sure have been blindsided, Bolen! Want to try that pass again?

Chapter 4

Never married! The last thing Kurt expected to hear. He'd figured Maddie merely used her maiden name professionally like a lot of women did today.

A thought popped into his head. Had the guy she was waiting for last night on Poorman's Peak fathered Scotty? Some bastard who had knocked her up then went home to his wife, kids and happy home? That could be why she was still single. She'd probably been having a running affair with the guy for the past ten years. He felt the rise of anger. And who ultimately pays the price—the kid!

Not your problem, Bolen, so move on.

He threw up his hands in defeat. "I've really heard more than I care to. This is none of my business."

He figured that was as good an exit line as any. So it was time to exit stage right. "Nice seeing you again, Maddie. Take care of Scotty. He's a great kid."

Maddie had struggled with how she should handle the

issue of Kurt Bolen. Her initial knee-jerk reaction when he had suddenly appeared in Vandergriff had been one of panic—the possibility that he would disrupt her world. She had gone as far as demonizing him to justify this fear. And then this same man had saved Scotty's life.

For the past nine years she'd been justified in raising Scotty without revealing the identity of his father—she'd had no idea whether Kurt Bolen was alive or dead. But now that he was here, even though he had no intention of remaining, was it fair to let him leave without telling him he had a son?

And if God had brought Kurt back for a reason, she had to face that reality and consider Scotty's needs—not her own, not Kurt Bolen's—but Scotty's.

She'd be blind if she didn't see how much her son worshipped this man already. Was it jealousy on her part to even struggle with the issue? Fear that she no longer would be the center of Scotty's devotion. Of course not. Scotty worshipped Aunt Beth, too. And besides, Scotty had so much love in his young heart, it was only natural for him to reach out to Kurt.

If only she knew more about Kurt. What he'd been up to in the past ten years. Married? Divorced? Other children?

There she was at it again. She wasn't the omnipotent being in the issue. It wasn't her decision. A power much greater than she had made the decision—and she had to have the faith to trust the outcome.

"Kurt, wait. Are you religious at all?"

"Enough to believe that whatever choices you make along the way will not change your destiny, whether you die young from an infected hangnail or in old age from senility."

She looked at him a moment then sighed. "Before you leave there's something I must tell you."

"Maddie, I don't want to know. I've heard all I want to hear. I'm just an ex-schoolmate passing through town. I'm not interested in hearing your family secrets, much less where the bodies are buried."

Maddie hesitated. He was giving her the excuse to ease her conscience if she let him leave without telling him. Then, once again, she reminded herself that this wasn't about her interests or Kurt's; this was about what was good for Scotty.

Maddie took a deep breath. "I think you might be interested in what I have to say. Kurt, you're Scotty's father."

Too stunned to speak, Kurt stared at her until he found his voice. "What in hell are you trying to pull, lady? Is this some kind of con to put a squeeze on me?"

"No, it's not. I just thought you should know. Please feel free to leave."

"You're damn right I'm leaving."

Kurt spun on his heel and headed back inside to get his pack. He got as far as the third step, then hesitated and came back.

"Why me? That story might have worked with other men, but I've never laid a hand on you, so why try it with me?"

"Kurt, I said you were free to leave. I struggled with telling you the truth from the time you showed up here. Now that I have, my conscience is clear and if you don't choose to believe me, at least I did put it out on the table."

"That must have been one hell of a struggle since it took you ten years to tell me."

"And how would I have done so sooner, when I had no idea where to find you?"

"I don't know why I'm even pursuing this argument. But for a starter, when I left town Joey knew I headed to Milwaukee to enlist in the navy."

"By the time I realized I was pregnant, Joey had left here himself. I didn't tell anyone the name of Scotty's father."

"You still could have tracked me down through the government. I wasn't in hiding."

Her eyes flashed angrily. "And if I had nothing better to do with my excessive wealth, I suppose I could have run a personal ad in *every* newspaper in the country, too—Kurt Bolen, all is forgiven. Come home and meet your son."

"You've got a good sell there, lady, but I'm not buying."

"Well, thank you again, for saving my son. I'm indebted to you for giving him to me ten years ago—and again today. Now, if you'll excuse me." She started to pass him, but his hand on her arm prevented her.

"Oh, you're good, baby. You're good! If I didn't know better, I'd start believing you myself. Why would you even try such a ridiculous scheme, when we both know nothing ever happened?"

"It happened," she said, and brushed aside his hand and opened the screen door.

"Like when? The world's already had one immaculate conception and I don't frequent sperm banks."

She turned her head, and her look was withering. "Try ten years ago, Kurt, on the night of our graduation."

The screen door slammed behind her.

Kurt followed her into the house. "What about the night of graduation?"

Maddie cast a stricken look at Beth. "I've said all I prefer to on the subject."

"Is that right? Well tough, lady. You don't drop a bombshell like this and then walk away. I want answers."

"It appears the two of you have an issue to resolve, so if you don't mind finishing the dishes, Maddie, I'll go to my room," Beth said. "Thank you again, Kurt, for what you did this morning, and if I don't see you again, good luck in the future."

"I'm not going anywhere," he said.

"You said you were leaving," Maddie accused.

For a long moment their determined gazes clashed, then Kurt looked at Beth. "That is if you have no objection, Beth."

"Of course not. I'll break the good news to Scotty." She hurried away.

"I knew it would be a mistake to tell you about Scotty," Maddie said, and began to put away the dishes.

"What do you expect? You opened this can of worms. Why wouldn't I want answers?"

"What difference does it make now? It happened ten years ago."

"If I'm to believe you, the *difference* is upstairs in his bedroom."

Frustrated, Maddie dropped a glass and it splintered. She bent down to pick up the pieces and in her haste she cut her finger. It began to bleed.

Kurt rushed over and turned on the faucet. "Get your finger under this cold water. Where's the disinfectant?"

"In the cabinet in the powder room."

"Keep your finger under that cold water until I get back."

He returned shortly with the tin of bandages and a bottle of disinfectant. "Let me take a look."

His hand was warm and incredibly gentle as he patted the finger dry with tissue and checked the cut. His nearness and the warmth of his touch gave an incredible sense of comfort— and an unexpected excitement.

It had been ten years since Maddie had been this aware of a man's touch—especially a man she'd been physically attracted to. And Lord knows, Kurt Bolen was physically attractive. Now, more than ever. She could well imagine the trail of broken hearts that followed him.

Don't even go there, Maddie.

She felt foolish as he sprayed on disinfectant. "I'm fine."

"Just the same, let's get a bandage on it to keep it clean."

He has beautiful hands, she thought as he pressed the gauze strip around the cut. Gentle, yet firm and comforting. His fingers were long and tan, the nails clipped and clean.

And his nearness still generated the same excitement she'd always felt around him. So close she could feel the heat of his body—yet so out of reach as if miles separated them.

Lord, Maddie, the man is a threat to life as you know it, so get over schoolgirl romanticizing.

He moved instinctively to the closet and came back with a broom and dustpan in hand. Within minutes he'd disposed of the shattered glass.

At least the accident had dissolved her anger and appeared to have done the same to his.

"Do you suppose we can sit down and discuss this situation like two sensible adults, Maddie?"

She chuckled. "If we'd done that ten years ago, we wouldn't be having this conversation. There's still some coffee left, are you interested?"

Kurt shook his head. "I could use a beer."

"Sorry, we don't have any."

He shoved back his chair and stood up. "Then how about a ride? I'm beginning to feel the walls closing in on me."

There was no traffic on the road, and the soft hum of the car and occasional chatter of starlings were the only sounds that invaded the quiet summer night.

Her life had become ludicrous. Nothing was normal anymore. How could she be sitting beside Kurt Bolen in the intimacy of a car, driving down the same road as if there hadn't been a lapse of ten years?

"How's your leg feeling?" she finally asked, breaking the silence between them.

"Fine. The pills killed the pain."

"Are you bothered often?"

"No. The leg rarely bothers me anymore."

"I didn't mean your leg. I meant your edginess, the feeling

of being confined, the walls closing in on you that you spoke of earlier."

"Is this your 101 Shrink class, Professor?"

"You're right. It's none of my business."

He drew a deep breath. "I'm sorry. Truth is I wouldn't last a week in a 9 to 5 office job if that's what you mean."

Whether by intention or not, they'd ended up at Poorman's Peak. He parked and turned off the engine.

"Aunt Beth said you told her you work for the government. What bureau?" she asked.

"I'm not here to talk about myself, Maddie. I want to know why you accused me of fathering Scotty."

"Kurt, let me make myself clear from the start. As far as Scotty goes, I'm not asking anything from you regarding responsibility or child support. I only told you what I did to clear my conscience."

"Drop all the bull and tell me why you accuse me of being Scotty's father when I never laid a hand on you."

It was obvious he was fighting to quell his irritation, so she took a deep breath and for the second time in as many evenings, Maddie relived the events of that long ago evening, avoiding only the embarrassing confession of the secret feelings she'd had for him at the time.

As she spoke, Kurt watched the changing expressions on her face. She was either the world's best actress or was telling him the truth—because he believed her. This was the nagging thing he hadn't been able to remember about her earlier. Fleeting images began to flicker in and out of his mind.

"I remember waking up the next morning in front of my shanty. So you drove me home that night."

"It was either that or leave you up here all night. You'd passed out and could have been charged with a DUI."

"So here's where Scotty was conceived." He glanced below at Stoneville. "Thank God you got him out of there, Maddie."

Kurt turned on the car and pulled out. He had a lot to think about—a lot of decisions to make. Maddie must have realized this, and was quiet on the ride back.

"I have to go back to the hospital tomorrow to get checked out, but then I'm coming back to work out some arrangement with you," Kurt said when they reached the house.

Don't panic. Stay calm, she warned herself. "Kurt, I meant what I said. I don't need or want your help. I've gotten along thus far without it. If you simply keep me informed of an address where you can be reached in the event of an emergency, there would be no reason for you to remain."

"I think that's not entirely your decision to make. Since I've just discovered I have a son, I'd like to spend some time with him. Maybe you should pass that question by Scotty, and see what he thinks."

So this was the start of his interference—the very reason she had hesitated to tell him. "I beg you, Kurt, please don't tell Scotty the truth until we work this out. He's the one who can be hurt by it all."

"What did you tell him about his father?"

"I told him his father left before he even knew I was going to have a baby."

"Well, thank you for that. At least you didn't make me sound like a child deserter."

"I did it so that Scotty would never think his father left because of him. I understand children often do so when their parents split up."

Maddie got out of the car and went into the house. As soon as Kurt locked the door behind them, she said goodnight and headed up the stairs.

"And, Maddie," Kurt said behind her, "I think Scotty should call me Kurt—unless you prefer Dad."

Chapter 5

Kurt followed Maddie up the stairs a short time later, but sleep was out of the question for him. A man doesn't find out he has a son and simply lie down and go to sleep. He stared at the sleeping boy in the other bed, and his heart swelled with tenderness. Scotty was a great kid, and he deserved a better father than Kurt could ever be. But he sure as hell was going to try and make up for a lot of lost years.

He had no idea how Scotty would react when they told the boy Kurt was his father. Trouble was, it was clear Maddie would bode no interference on his part, so who was going to be the biggest problem—the mother or the son?

He figured he'd go back to Milwaukee in the morning, get his final checkup, and then come back and spend the rest of his leave in Vandergriff. Dave Cassidy was a lawyer, and once Kurt and Maddie settled on an arrangement, he'd have Dave draw up a new will. In the event the squad had to go on another mission, he wanted to be certain Scotty and Maddie were his beneficiaries.

It was three o'clock by the time Kurt finally fell asleep. Scotty's cries awoke him a short time later. The boy was sitting up in bed crying. Kurt jumped to his feet and ran over to him. Trembling with fright, Scotty clutched at him.

"Hey, buddy, what's wrong?" Kurt murmured, embracing him.

"Don't let go of me," Scotty sobbed.

Kurt tightened his arms around him. "I won't, pal. Did you have a bad dream?"

"I was in this big pool of black water, and…and I was choking and couldn't breathe."

"You were reliving your accident, Scotty. You're fine, there's nothing to be afraid of."

"Will you stay with me, Mr. Bolen?"

"Sure will. I won't let anything happen to you. And you can call me Kurt. Your mother said it was okay."

The boy looked up at him, tears streaking his cheeks. "Promise?"

"Promise, buddy. And you never break a promise to a buddy."

Scotty stopped crying and wiped his eyes with a balled fist. "Am I really your buddy?"

"If you want to be."

"I sure want to be. I bet you're the best buddy a fella could have."

"Hey, I was thinking the same thing about you."

"Do you have other buddies?"

"Only older ones," Kurt said. "The guys in my…guys I work with. What about you?"

"I've got a couple friends at school, but I don't have a real buddy."

"Well, you've got one now. Tell you what, tomorrow I have to go into Milwaukee to get my leg checked, then I'll come back and we'll pal around together until I have to go back to work. Would you like that?"

"Really! Oh, boy, wait until I tell Mom!"

"Can you swim, Scotty?"

He hung his head. "Not very good. I'm kind of afraid of the water."

"I bet I could teach you how to swim so good that you'd never be afraid of water again."

"Could you really?"

"Yeah, I'm a pretty good swimmer."

Scotty leaned forward. "Do you think you could teach my mom?" he asked in a half whisper. "She's afraid of water, too."

"If she'll let me." So, like mother, like son. "Now, how about you going back to sleep. Do you want a drink of water?"

Scotty giggled. "No, sir. I drank all the water today I want to." Scotty slipped his hand into Kurt's. "Will you stay with me until I fall asleep?"

"I promise, buddy."

"And a buddy never breaks a promise to a buddy," Scotty said. Smiling, he lay back and closed his eyes. "It's sure gonna be nice having a buddy like you."

Kurt sat on the edge of the bed, holding his son's hand until Scotty fell asleep.

As soon as she heard Scotty cry out, Maddie bolted from her bed and rushed to his bedroom. She paused in the doorway when she saw him sitting up and clutching Kurt. For some inexplicable reason she chose to remain silent and not intrude on the scene.

As she listened to them, she could see how much Scotty missed and needed to have an adult male in his life. She had concentrated so hard on making a life for him that she had neglected the one thing he needed the most—a father to comfort him, to teach him the things a boy learns from just being around a man—especially around a father.

And it was obvious that he and Kurt had bonded from the beginning. Even just now, no matter how frightened Scotty had been, not once had he cried out for her.

She struggled with the reality that at this stage of his life Scotty needed Kurt more than he did her. She thought her heart would break, and turned away and went back to her room.

Unable to fall back to sleep, Maddie got up and went downstairs to have a cup of tea. To her surprise, Beth had already brewed a pot and filled two mugs.

"I was just coming upstairs to your room. I thought it's time we had a talk," Beth said.

"Aunt Beth, it's almost four o'clock."

"And neither of us are ready to go to sleep, so this is as good a time as any."

Maddie was too emotionally drained to put up an argument. She sat down and took a sip of the hot brew.

"Kurt is Scotty's father, isn't he?" Beth said.

Maddie took another sip of the tea. She needed something to fortify her for this conversation. "When did you realize it?"

"I suspected it by your bizarre reaction to him at the diner. This morning at the quarry my suspicions were confirmed when I had a better opportunity to see them together. The resemblance is obvious."

Beth reached over and grasped Maddie's hand. "Honey, if ever two people belonged together it's your son and his father. How can you deny it any longer?"

Maddie drew a shuddering breath. "I can't. I realize that now. Aunt Beth, believe me, I didn't deliberately keep them apart. I had no idea where to find Kurt when I discovered I was pregnant. But I didn't try to find him, for which I now must bear the guilt. And then with my folks and Joey getting killed, there was just too much coming at me at the same time, so I gave up any thought of finding Kurt."

"So why are you trying to drive him away now?"

"Because he's a threat to me. After all this time, he suddenly appears and threatens the life I've worked so hard to achieve."

"Honey, you know I love you like a daughter, and no one is as aware as I what you've gone through raising him. But so far all I've heard is about you. What about Scotty? What about Kurt? Don't you think they have needs, too? You can't play God with people's lives, Maddie."

"I realize that, but I can't just shove aside the past ten years as if they'd never existed, either. I've got to have more time to think through this whole situation. I know nothing about this man, and to encourage the relationship without knowing could be just as harmful to Scotty as denying him the truth."

"I think it's too late for that choice. Like it or not, it's out of your hands now." Beth rose to her feet. "Trust in the Almighty, honey. The ball's back in His court now." She kissed Maddie on the cheek and went back upstairs.

Kurt could feel the intensity of the stare before he even opened his eyes. He started to accumulate his thoughts as last night's startling revelation flooded his memory. He opened his eyes to find Scotty standing at his bedside, grinning widely.

"Good morning, Kurt."

"Morning," Kurt replied.

He didn't feel any more like a father than he had when he awoke yesterday morning. Yet he liked the idea. It gave him a sense of being worthwhile. Other than the contribution he made as a member of the Dwarf Squad, he really had somewhat of a aimless life—no strings, no commitments.

And that had been just fine—until now.

"Mom said you've got fifteen minutes to shower and dress, unless you like cold pancakes."

"She did, did she? Have you eaten yet?"

"No, we waited for you."

Kurt bolted to his feet. "Then I guess I better hurry."

"Yeah, 'cause Mom said *that* five minutes ago."

Twelve minutes later Kurt entered the kitchen—showered, shaved and dressed; he'd learned how to move fast in the military.

His stomach growled a welcome to the smell of coffee and fried bacon. Maddie was at the stove flipping pancakes and Scotty was seated at the table with a knife in one hand and a fork in the other. The domestic sight was enough to warm even the heart of a confirmed bachelor like him.

"Good morning"

Maddie turned and smiled faintly. "Good morning. Did you sleep well?"

"Pretty good except for the loud snorer in the next bed."

Scotty giggled. "I don't snore." Then with that edge of self-doubt Kurt had noticed before, Scotty asked, "Do I, Mom?"

"I was only joking, buddy. I slept like a log."

"Well, sit down. Breakfast is ready." She placed a platter of pancakes and bacon on the table.

Kurt gulped down a glass of orange juice, then poured himself a cup of coffee. He needed that caffeine fix.

"Where's Beth this morning?"

"She and Mrs. Jennings went to Milwaukee," Scotty said.

"There's an international medical symposium in progress," Maddie said. "Dr. Fernando Escobar, a doctor whose career Beth's followed with great respect, is one of the speakers. She and Adele Jennings are retired nurses, so they decided to attend."

"That's the same guy we heard on television yesterday. Isn't it, Kurt?" Scotty said.

He nodded. "Yeah, small world, isn't it?" Smaller than you think. He didn't mention Colombia to them.

"Wish I would have known. I could have driven them."

"They're gone for the next couple days."

Scotty's eyes widened. "Are you really coming back?"

"Didn't I say I would? I've thought it over and I've decided to return to my roots." He glanced at Maddie. She didn't look happy.

"Hooray!" Scotty shouted, oblivious to the two people staring intensely across the table at one another.

"I…ah, thought your home was in D.C.," Maddie said.

"It is but it's just a small apartment. It'll be no trouble to move."

"What about your job? Don't you work there?"

"I travel a lot with my job, so it doesn't make any difference."

"Now that you're gonna move here, you can teach me to swim," Scotty said. "Mom, Kurt said he'd teach you, too."

"You bet." Kurt glanced at Maddie. She was staring into space, the food forgotten on her plate.

He knew damn well what she was thinking.

Maddie got up from the table and began to fuss at the sink with the dishes.

"You haven't finished eating, Maddie."

"I'm not hungry. Besides, it's time to open the store."

"What kind of store is it?"

"I have a small bookstore."

"In the strip mall?" She nodded. "I saw it when I drove in the other day." He got up and carried his plate to the sink. "Yeah, I should be getting on my way, too. I have an appointment."

"Scotty, Melanie's on vacation and with Aunt Beth gone, you're going to have to spend the day at the store."

The boy's shoulders drooped. "Ah, Mom, that's so boring."

"I'll take care of him," Kurt said. "He can drive into Milwaukee with me. Once my final examination is over, I'm on my own. We can do the town." He winked at Scotty. "Right, buddy."

"Oh, boy! Can I, Mom?" Scotty asked.

"I don't think that's a good idea, honey. After all, we barely know Kurt, and…it would be imposing on him."

"Not at all. Why don't you come with us?"

"I can't—I mean it's impossible. I have a business to run. I closed up early yesterday as it was."

All the stuttering and stammering she was doing didn't fool Kurt for a moment. The simple truth was that she didn't trust for Scotty to be alone with him. "So the sky won't fall if you close up today, too."

"Yeah, Mom, please," Scotty said. "We never do anything like that."

"I planned on taking inventory today before—"

"Please, Mom?" Scotty pleaded. "Maybe after Kurt's through with his examination, we can go to the zoo."

"Yeah, Mom, we can go to the zoo," Kurt said, tongue in cheek.

Kurt figured if looks could kill, Maddie just launched an RPG at him. Fortunately he'd dodged enough of those rocket propelled grenades to know how to duck. And he sensed this situation was building up to combat. Time to negotiate.

"Scotty, why don't you go upstairs and make your bed while I talk to your mother?"

"I don't know how to make my bed."

"Time you learn. I'll come up in a minute and show you how it's done in the military."

"Oh, boy!" Scotty raced out of the room.

"You don't trust me, do you, Maddie? If you feel you can't come, I'll take an oath not to run off with him."

"I didn't mean to imply that. I just wouldn't feel comfortable sending him off. I've never done it before."

"Then come with us. When was the last time you did something just for the fun of it?"

"I have responsibilities."

"One day's not going to bankrupt you, and you wouldn't want to disappoint Scotty. The kid's all wired to go."

Maddie sighed deeply. "I guess the decision's out of my hands."

"Are you coming up?" Scotty yelled from the top of the stairway.

Kurt grinned. "I think he means me." He headed upstairs.

For the next ten minutes, Kurt showed Scotty how to make up his bed. "Tomorrow, you do it yourself. Make sure those corners are squared, sailor, and you can bounce a coin off the top."

Scotty saluted. "Aye, aye, sir."

When they went downstairs, Maddie had the kitchen in order and was ready to go.

Scotty was so excited he talked practically the whole two-hour drive to Milwaukee. Kurt couldn't help grinning. But at least the kid had waited until they were out of the county before asking if they were almost there.

Chapter 6

The veterans' hospital was in the immediate vicinity of Miller Park, home of the Milwaukee Brewers baseball team. Scotty was ecstatic when he saw the huge sliding dome of the stadium's structure.

"Wow! Look at that!"

"The Brewers are playing the Cubs tonight. What say we forget about the zoo and take in the game?" Kurt said. "We can always come back and do the zoo some other day."

"Oh, boy! Can we? I've never been to a *real* baseball game."

There he goes again, just as I suspected, Maddie thought. Taking over. Making plans with her son without asking or consulting her. And the situation will only get worse if Kurt moves back to Vandergriff, which he apparently intended to do.

This latest suggestion was ludicrous and too spontaneous. She stole a glance at Kurt as he pulled into the parking lot of the facility. The man was worse than a child! "Are you suggesting we stay in Milwaukee over night?"

"Sure."

"We just can't stay overnight without coming prepared to do so," she declared.

"What's stopping us?"

"A change of clothing for one thing."

"Malls are full of clothing stores," he said.

"Have you forgotten I have a business to run?"

"We can be back tomorrow morning in plenty of time to open your store."

The man had an answer for everything.

Maddie turned her head to look at Scotty, who had been unusually quiet during the whole discussion. He had his eyes closed and was holding both hands up with the fingers crossed. Motherhood was becoming more difficult by the moment—since she now had *two* children to contend with.

"I see I'm already outvoted, but it's a stupid idea."

"Do you have a cell phone?" Kurt asked.

"Yes."

"Do you know where Beth's registered?"

"The symposium is being held at the convention center."

"That's in downtown Milwaukee. We're west of it right now. When I'm through here, we can go downtown and maybe have an early dinner with her if she doesn't have other plans. There's a mall nearby and we can pick up whatever you and Scotty need. While I'm checking out here, call Beth, and book us a couple of rooms at the same hotel." He reached in his pocket and pulled out his wallet. "Here's my credit card."

She took it with no qualms. "Since this is your brilliant idea, I *will* let you pick up the tab. Any more orders, General?"

He grinned. "If I were an officer, it would be Admiral, honey. I was in the navy." He got out of the car. "Here's the keys. I shouldn't be too long. What's your cell phone number? I'll call you when I'm ready to leave."

She wrote down the number. "Isn't it risky giving me your

car keys. I could be halfway back to Vandergriff by the time you're through."

"My buddy wouldn't let you do that." He looked at Scotty's mile-wide grin. "A buddy looks out for his buddy's interests. Right, pal?"

"Aye, aye, Admiral."

Kurt winked and hurried off.

"What did he mean by all that 'buddy' talk?" Maddie asked.

"Kurt and I are buddies, Mom. And a buddy never lets his buddy down," Scotty said solemnly.

"Can't a mom be a buddy?"

"Oh, no. Guys can be buddies, but, mom's are very, very special. 'Bout the most special people in the whole world."

"Is that what your *buddy* said?"

"No, that's what I said."

Maddie smiled, and tousled his hair.

She wanted to hug and kiss him. Being a mom wasn't so bad, after all. It had some very precious moments. "Come on, you little munchkin. Let's get out and stretch our legs. I'll call Aunt Beth, and then we'll look around at this place."

Beth was delighted to hear they were in town and said she'd take care of reserving them rooms for the night. They agreed to meet for dinner.

Her business now completed, Maddie and Scotty walked around the huge grounds of the facility, which not only was a hospital but a residence for many of the handicapped veterans.

A military cemetery with rows upon rows of white crosses stretched out on the grassy knoll of the facility, the final resting place for the hundreds of Wisconsin's sons who had paid the ultimate price for their country's freedom in past wars.

They had no sooner returned to the car, then Kurt rejoined them and they drove to downtown Milwaukee. The city was bordered on the east by Lake Michigan, and they strolled along the beach, then spread out a blanket and sat down to relax while Scotty started to build a sand castle.

"So did you get a clean bill of health on your leg?" Maddie felt uncomfortable. In truth, this man was a comparative stranger to her. But they had a son in common that forced a bond between them whether she liked it or not.

"Yeah, the doc said it's looking good. It'll be fit as a fiddle in no time." He chuckled. The warm sound of it made her smile. "I never understood what a fiddle has to do with being fit."

"How soon before you go back to work?"

"The doctor said thirty days."

"What exactly do you do, Kurt?" Maddie asked.

"Hey, Mom," Scotty yelled, "look at my castle."

"Looks great, sweetheart," she called back. She turned back to Kurt and smiled. "He's really enjoying himself."

"So am I. He's a great kid."

"He's very attached to you already. What happens when the novelty wears off, Kurt, and you get tired of playing Dad? Do you break his heart when you up and leave?"

"What makes you think I'll leave him?"

"You couldn't wait to leave ten years ago. I'm sure you'll find Vandergriff just as dull as you did then."

"Get over it. I'm no longer that eighteen-year-old, Maddie. I've learned a lot these past ten years. Ever think that maybe you're the one who hasn't grown up?"

He got up and started to walk along the shoreline. Scotty abandoned his sand castle and chased after him.

Maddie's gaze followed them. She didn't know how to handle Kurt Bolen. How could she *not* judge him by the person he was ten years ago? What other guidelines did she have? In the past ten years she had never held a bitter thought toward him. He had given her the most precious gift she could ever hope for. But now she was afraid to trust him—he threatened her life.

When they left the beach, they made a stop at the Grand Avenue Mall for toiletries and a change of underclothing. Then they registered at the hotel in time to freshen up and go downstairs to join Beth for dinner.

Beth and Adele Jennings were seated at a table with none other than the symposium's keynote speaker, Dr. Fernando Escobar. Kurt recognized him at once.

"Adele and I had been to Dr. Escobar's hospital in Colombia a couple years ago with a volunteer medical team," Beth informed them after the introductions were made.

"Yes, once again I have the pleasure of the company of these two beautiful ladies," Escobar said.

"Wow! I saw you on television. Now I'm meeting you in person," Scotty said. "I told my mom if I die that I want my organs donated to help other kids."

Dr. Escobar appeared amused. "That is most generous of you, young man." He turned to Kurt. "You look vaguely familiar, Mr. Bolen. Have we met before?"

"Yes, sir."

"I apologize for my lapse of memory. Where was it?"

"In Colombia, sir." Kurt wanted to drop the subject. He knew it would only lead to having to make explanations to Maddie later. But the doctor pursued his questioning.

"Are you in the medical profession, Mr. Bolen?"

"No, sir."

Escobar appeared perplexed. "When was the occasion?"

"It was a year ago, sir," Kurt replied, trying to hedge the answer.

"Kurt works for the American government," Beth volunteered.

"Oh, so you are in the diplomatic service, Mr. Bolen."

Now, all eyes were fixed on him, waiting for his reply. "Not exactly. It involved some detained Americans."

Escobar's expression suddenly changed. "Of course, now

I remember. You were a member of a team that rescued the American hostages being held by terrorists."

"Yes, sir." Kurt glanced at Maddie. She looked startled and was staring at him with her mouth agape.

"You had a couple patients who'd been victims of organ harvesting," Kurt said, hoping to change the subject. "Did they recover, Doctor?"

"Yes, fully. Both are doing well today."

"That's good," Kurt said. "I saw in today's newspaper that the police found a suspected organ harvesting victim right here in Milwaukee. The man is still unconscious, so they hadn't had a chance to question him."

"Oh my, the poor man!" Beth exclaimed. "I hope it's not true. Why do the police suspect he's a victim of such a crime? Wouldn't his family know if such a thing were true?"

"According to the article the man was homeless, and to date, no family member has stepped forward. Coincidence isn't it, Doctor?"

"What is?" Escobar asked.

"I'd never encountered a victim of organ harvesting until Colombia, and now one shows up here. You must be the attraction, Doctor."

Escobar gave him a wary look, then smiled. "I certainly hope not, Mr. Bolen." He glanced at his watch. "Forgive me, ladies, but I must rush off."

"But you haven't eaten, Doctor," Beth said.

"I must apologize, but I just remembered I have an important meeting to attend. Elizabeth and Adele, I will see you later." He stood up. "It was a pleasure to meet you and your son, Ms. Bennett." Kurt stood up to shake his hand. "And to meet again, young man, under these more pleasant circumstances."

The guy was too smooth, Kurt thought. The doctors he'd encountered were less on charm and heavier on business. Of course they'd all been in the military and didn't have to stroke their patients. Could just be the man's continental manners. But why the quick exit? Something stunk like three-day-old fish.

Maddie was quiet throughout the meal, but whenever he glanced at her, she had that uptight look again. There'd be no avoiding the explanation she was waiting to hear.

Fortunately, Beth and Adele remained with them until it was time to leave for the game. It was a hot night, so the stadium's roof was open, and it wasn't any different than watching a game under the stars. The Brewers had a three-run lead by the bottom of the eighth inning when Scotty announced he had to use the men's room.

Scotty went into the men's room, and while Kurt waited he walked over to a vending bar and ordered a beer for himself and Cokes for Scotty and Maddie. He noticed a man lingering around the door of the men's room. He didn't like the guy's body language, and his instincts kicked in. He started to walk over to the door and the guy turned abruptly and walked away. Scotty came out just then, and Kurt said, "Did you wash your hands?"

"Hey, you sound just like Mom."

A big roar sounded from the crowd, and Kurt handed him one of the Cokes. "Let's get back to that game."

The Cubs had scored four runs in the top of the ninth, and the home team was now up to bat. They failed to score in the bottom of the ninth.

The fact that the Brewers lost the game did not diminish Scotty's enthusiasm, especially when Kurt bought him a Brewers' cap and pennant on the way out. They returned to the hotel and said good-night.

He had dodged a bullet by not having to give Maddie an explanation about his job. But tomorrow was another day.

Beth joined them for breakfast the next morning. Scotty was silent and picked at his food throughout the meal.

"What's the matter, sweetheart?" Maddie asked. "Aren't you feeling well?"

"I'm okay," he murmured.

"Don't you like your breakfast, honey?" Beth asked.

"It's fine, Aunt Beth."

Maddie put a hand on his forehead. "He doesn't feel feverish. But something's wrong. What is it?"

Scotty cast a woeful glance at Kurt, who had already figured out the boy's problem. "Mom, as long as we're here, why can't we stay another day and go to the zoo?"

"We've been through all that yesterday. I have a business to run, a store mortgage to pay off—and the responsibility of feeding that insatiable appetite of yours, which seems to be lacking this morning."

"Will a couple days make *that* much difference, Maddie?" Kurt asked. "How many books can you sell in the course of a day in Vandergriff?"

She gave him an officious look. "Trying to reason with a nine-year-old is difficult enough so I don't need any interference from you, Kurt. I not only sell books, I sell newspapers, magazines and have a connecting tea room that offers beverage, soup, a cold sandwich and a dessert. That's a big part of my income."

Maddie worked hard to earn a living, he'd give her credit for that. But if she didn't climb down from that high horse she'd soon discover the real meaning of interference from him. Scotty was his son, too. He wasn't going to spoil the day by butting heads with her. "So who prepares the food, Ms. Bennett?"

She must have realized he was going to let it slide. She gave him a contrite glance and her tone softened. "Beth usually helps me. In the summer, I hire a college student part-time to give me a hand. It's only open between eleven and two in the afternoons, and the local reading group meets there every Thursday for lunch and their weekly meeting. Every little bit helps, you know."

"Well, this is only Tuesday. You won't be upsetting anyone's applecart," Kurt said lightly.

"Please, Mom," Scotty said. "Please."

Maddie glanced at his eager expression and threw her hands up in defeat. "I suppose one more day won't make that much difference." It got her a big kiss and hug from Scotty and a wide grin from Kurt.

Beth's reaction was as eager as Scotty's. "Well, that's delightful. And we can meet again for dinner tonight."

"Is that agreeable to you, Kurt?" Maddie asked.

"I'm cool with it. Since we aren't checking out this morning, I'll see if our rooms are available for another night."

Scotty jumped to his feet. "I'll go with you."

"I'm afraid I'm spoiling him," Maddie said woefully as she watched Kurt and her son disappear.

Beth reached over and patted her hand. "No you're not. Scotty's a happy little boy, honey, and for the first time in his young life he's enjoying a new experience—a man in his life. He doesn't want it to end."

Maddie glanced worriedly at her aunt. "And what happens when the bubble bursts, Aunt Beth? You know it will when Kurt gets bored with playing father and walks out on him."

"I know no such thing, and neither do you. Are you forgetting this is as much of a shock to Kurt as it is to you? Why don't you give the man the benefit of believing that he has Scotty's interests at heart as much as you do?"

"I just don't want to see Scotty hurt."

"Or yourself."

"The only way Kurt Bolen could ever hurt me is through Scotty."

Beth smiled slyly. "You keep telling yourself that, dear, but you're not fooling me for a minute. I think it's about time you have a man in your life—and what better choice than the father of your son."

"That's ludicrous, Aunt Beth. Now you're really talking nonsense," she declared as Kurt and Scotty entered the room. "Look at them, Aunt Beth. Two peas in a pod. They even look alike—Kurt and Mini-Kurt. Wouldn't you be scared if you were me?"

"Not a chance, honey. If I had it to do over again and a man like Kurt Bolen entered my life, he'd be welcomed with open arms."

Maddie realized she had given little thought as to why her aunt had remained single. Physically, Beth had always been an attractive woman with a pleasant disposition. Surely she must have had offers of marriage.

"Were you ever in love, Aunt Beth?"

Beth looked at her and smiled. "Of course, honey."

Kurt sat down before Beth could say more. "We're cool."

Scotty gave Maddie a big hug. "You're the bestest mom in the whole world."

"And don't you ever forget it, munchkin," Maddie murmured, giving Kurt a challenging glance over the boy's shoulder. It appeared to have no effect on him. Undaunted, and looking pleased with himself, he leaned back with a self-satisfied grin on that damn good-looking face of his.

"I better get moving," Beth said. "Today's session is about to begin. Where should we meet for dinner?"

"How about me taking all of you out to a fancy restaurant tonight?" Kurt said.

Maddie shook her head. "No fancy restaurants, please. We aren't dressed for it. Right here will be fine. Is seven o'clock okay for you, Aunt Beth?"

"Yes. The session today ends at five. I can get in a short nap before dinner. This city life is exhausting." She got up to leave. "By the way, I hope you won't have any objection if Dr. Escobar joins us. I promised to have dinner with him."

"Not at all," Maddie said. "What about Adele?"

"She has family here and has made dinner plans with them. Enjoy the zoo, my darlings." She hurried away.

Kurt perused the zoo pamphlet the desk clerk had given him. "Looks like we're in for a lot of walking. You two need anything from your room before we go?" Kurt asked.

"Hey, what happened to my plate?" Scotty suddenly questioned.

"The waitress took it," Maddie said.

"I wasn't through, Mom. How do you 'spect me to go to the zoo when I'm still hungry!"

Scotty's sudden declaration took Maddie by surprise and she fought back a grin. "I don't 'spect you to go hungry, Mr. Scott Joseph Bennett, but from the way you were picking at your food, I had the impression you weren't hungry."

"I wasn't hungry then, but I am now. Besides, didn't you always tell me that breakfast is the most important meal of the day and I shouldn't go out without it?"

"I guess I did."

The kid was nobody's fool. Kurt winked at Maddie, then raised his hand and motioned to the waitress.

Chapter 7

A short time later with a full stomach and bubbling with excitement, all Scotty could talk about was last night's baseball game as they drove to the zoo.

"I had to practically arm wrestle him to get that cap off him last night," Maddie said. "He wanted to sleep with it on."

"Don't you have any other caps?" Kurt asked. "No Green Bay Packers? Milwaukee Bucks? Wisconsin Badgers?"

"No."

"Not even a Little League one?"

"I don't belong to Little League," Scotty said. "I don't know how to play baseball."

"Every boy's born knowing how to play baseball," Kurt declared. He gave Maddie a disgruntled glance, and she looked away to avoid making eye contact with him. Was she trying to turn the kid into a priss? It was another reminder to him of how much his son needed some male influence in his young life.

He yanked the brim of the cap down over Scotty's nose. "Looks like that's another thing we're going to have to tackle, pal," he said as he pulled into the parking lot.

Maddie had made up her mind not to let her earlier reservations spoil their day at the zoo. How could she? Scotty's enthusiasm boiled over onto both her and Kurt.

They were able to watch sea lions and polar bears as the animals swam underwater in glass-enclosed tanks. They strolled through the aviary with rare birds flying overhead, and rode a train around the whole park.

Maddie and Kurt laughed with delight as Scotty waved at them from the back of the camel he was riding or fed corn to the lambs and baby goats in the petting pens. Following their awestruck son, they viewed with pleasure such exotic animals as red pandas and snow leopards.

At noon, they paused and ate hot dogs covered with relish and mustard. Maddie opted for a bottle of water while Kurt and Scotty drank sodas, then they topped off their luncheon with ice cream bars.

Loathing the sight of snakes, alligators and other such reptiles, Maddie waited outside on a bench while Kurt and Scotty toured the reptile sanctuary.

By the time they finished their tour of all the fabulous varieties of animals Maddie was exhausted.

"I think we better get going," she said.

"Mom, can we go back and look at the macaques one more time?" Scotty pleaded.

"All right, but that's it," she declared.

She collapsed in relief on a bench as they watched the hilarious antics of the monkeys from Japan who romped freely on their open-air island.

"I gotta go to the toilet," Scotty said, and raced up a nearby hill to a comfort station.

Kurt came over and sat down next to her and she watched sympathetically as he started to massage his knee and thigh.

"I imagine after all this walking, your leg's pretty painful."

"Just slows me up a little bit."

"Well, I'm exhausted," Maddie said. "I must be getting too old for motherhood."

"Sure you are. What are you now, an old lady of twenty-six or twenty-seven?"

"I'm twenty-seven. Joey and I were a year apart."

"How come you graduated with us?"

"When we moved to Vandergriff they tested me and put me in the senior class."

"Oh, so you're a brain."

She snorted. "Hardly."

Kurt chuckled. Maddie liked the sound of it. It was warm and gave her a feeling of serenity. She leaned back and sighed.

"As tired as I am, I'm glad we came."

"I'm glad, too. Scotty's sure enjoying it."

After several more minutes of companionable relaxation, she glanced at her watch. "What's keeping that boy?"

"I'll go and check."

She felt a twinge of guilt as she watched Kurt walk away. The grassy knoll was steep, and his step was slower than before. It was obvious he was in more pain than he was willing to admit.

But it felt good to have a man lend a helping hand for a change. For nine years she had struggled to give Scotty the best upbringing she could. Maybe Kurt's appearance would be more positive than she once thought. Maybe…just maybe…she and Kurt could work out a successful relationship that would benefit all three of them.

As Kurt hurried toward the building he thought of how pleasant the last couple days had been. Here he was, twenty-eight years old and had never suspected what he'd been

missing. Despite how uptight and overprotective of Scotty
Maddie appeared at times, she was a good sport. And right or
wrong, her intentions were not selfish, but always what she
believed to be the best for Scotty. If they weren't she would
have let him drive away without knowing he had a son.

Dammit! No matter how hard he tried, he couldn't
remember clearly all the details of the night he'd made love
to her—if he wanted to consider knocking her up in a drunken
stupor as making love! He sure as hell would like another
proper shot at it. But despite how well they were getting along
these past couple days, he could tell Maddie was still uneasy
about him. So he wasn't going to try and hit on her. Besides,
there was still that mystery man in the picture, whom she'd
been waiting for on Poorman's Bluff the other night.

As he neared the building Kurt saw a man outside the
entrance. He looked vaguely familiar. The man glanced
around him then started to open the door. The guy's body
language made Kurt suspicious, then he realized the man re-
sembled the one he'd seen at the baseball stadium. Coincidence? Hell, no!

"Hey, hold up there," Kurt yelled.

The man spun around and when he saw Kurt he broke into
a run and dashed away into some nearby trees.

Scotty came out just as Kurt was about to enter. "You,
okay, Scotty?"

"Sure. What's wrong?"

"Just get back to your mother right away," Kurt yelled as
he ran into the trees in pursuit of the fleeing man.

The other side of the grove of trees opened up onto a walk.
There were several dozen people viewing the cages and pens,
but the man he'd been chasing was not among them. Disgusted
that he'd lost the guy, Kurt returned to Maddie and Scotty.

"What's wrong, Kurt?" Maddie asked. "Scotty said you
were chasing after a man."

He saw no sense in alarming her any more than she appeared to be already. "False alarm, I thought it was someone I knew."

Her dubious stare told him she didn't buy his explanation, but she turned away. As they headed back to the parking lot his thoughts were on the man he'd been chasing. He'd swear it was the same guy. If the man was a pedophile, it was hard to believe he had taken such a yen for Scotty as to follow them back to the hotel last night and then to the zoo today. The guy would have to be pretty sick to go to that much trouble. Of course, the bastard wouldn't be a pedophile if he wasn't pretty far gone already. And what better place to encounter a young kid then at a baseball game or the zoo?

Kurt shook the thought aside. Maybe it wasn't the same man he'd seen last night. Maybe it was some poor sucker at the wrong place at the wrong time who took off when he saw a crazy guy bearing down on him.

Keep it up, Bolen, and you'll be the one who ends up behind bars.

Upon returning to the hotel, Maddie and Scotty went to their room, but Kurt stopped off at the gift shop to purchase a newspaper to read the current box scores in the sports section.

Once in his room he sat down on the bed, took off his shoes and then removed the ankle holster he wore on his right leg. For a long moment he stared at the Springfield XD 40 caliber pistol. He had no need to wear it while he was on medical leave, but he sure as hell wasn't going to leave it behind in a hotel room where it might be stolen.

Placing the weapon on the bed table, Kurt grabbed the newspaper and stretched out.

An article on the front page regarding the organ harvesting victim caught his attention. The police had officially declared it a homicide investigation since the victim, Jacob Waring, died minutes after regaining consciousness. The homeless, forty-five-year-old Waring lived long enough to inform them of his identity, but recalled nothing after passing out in the alley.

The article went on with the few details the police had assembled, and ended with the usual request for anyone who may have witnessed or knew of anything regarding the investigation to contact them.

Kurt yawned, put aside the newspaper and closed his eyes. For some reason he fixated on this organ harvesting business. Why? he wondered as he dozed off. He woke up just in time for a quick shower before dinner.

The Bennett family and Dr. Escobar were already seated when Kurt joined them in the dining room. "Hope I haven't kept you waiting long."

"Not at all," Beth said with her usual graciousness. "We've just sat down ourselves."

"I started reading the newspaper and fell asleep."

"The newspaper is the best sleeping pill there is," Maddie said. "By the time you read it, you've already heard the news on television."

"Actually there was a very interesting article in it regarding that organ harvesting victim. He regained consciousness long enough to identify himself before he died."

"He died!"

The startled exclamation had come from Escobar. "Yes, sir. According to the article, the only thing this Waring remembered was some guy sitting down next to him in an alley and offering him a drink from a whiskey bottle."

"And he died before he could tell them anything else?"

"At least that's what the police claimed, Dr. Escobar," Kurt replied.

Escobar appeared visibly shaken. "It's unusual for a donor to die as a result of the surgery. Normally, the critical part of the procedure is to the recipient."

"I remember in Colombia, Fernando, when I had the pleasure of observing you do a kidney transplant," Beth said. "Your skill and composure when the patient flatlined were incredible. None of us who witnessed it believed the man would survive. Dr. Cramer told me afterward that the surgical team felt no other doctor could have reacted as quickly as you did. The man's alive today due to your skill, Fernando."

"I'm afraid not, my dear Beth. The man was killed six months later while holding up a liquor store."

"Have you performed many organ transplants, Doctor?"

"Many, Mr. Bolen." He smiled. "But fortunately the one Beth just described was the only one where the patient literally died from an unanticipated complication."

"What about *removal* of organs, Doctor? Have you performed many of those types of surgery?"

For a long moment Escobar regarded Kurt with a wary stare. "Organs, bones, arteries…babies, breasts and bullets. There isn't too much I haven't removed from the human body at one time or the other, Mr. Bolen."

"Too bad," Kurt said.

"Your point being?"

"Just think, Doctor, if you had removed Waring's kidney, the poor sucker might be alive today."

Escobar's glare clashed with the mockery in Kurt's stare.

"For goodness' sake," Maddie exclaimed, "can't we get off this morbid subject? It's not exactly my choice for a dinner appetizer."

Kurt contributed little to the conversation during the meal. Quite often in the course of the evening he felt Escobar's adversarial stare. There was no doubt he had made an enemy.

So what if he didn't fit into polite society. Something about Escobar didn't sit well with him. That three-day-old fish had definitely overstayed its welcome.

* * *

The following morning they checked out of the hotel and headed back to Vandergriff. Kurt turned off the interstate for gas and as he filled the tank he noticed a dark blue Mercedes pull up and idle nearby. When he returned to the highway, the blue car followed. His instinct kicked in again when fifteen minutes later that same car still hung back behind them.

He slowed his speed, and the blue car did the same. The itch at his nape got itchier. Not wanting to sound paranoid, he didn't tell Maddie his suspicions and continued on for another ten minutes. He could push his Charger up to a hundred and sixty if he wanted to and easily lose the car, but he wasn't about to take any risks with Maddie and Scotty in the car.

A short time later Scotty gave him the excuse he was hoping for. "Mom, I have to pee."

"Scotty, I told you to use the restroom at the gas station before we got back on the road."

"I didn't have to go then."

Swallowing a sigh Maddie said, "I'm sorry, Kurt, I guess we'll have to stop."

"No problem. I could use a pit stop, too. We'll pull into the next rest stop."

As soon as they pulled off the road, Scotty dashed to the men's room. Kurt dallied, and the blue Mercedes drove past. There were two men in the front seat.

He relaxed. So he'd been paranoid again—one of the hazards of his job. Shrugging aside his suspicions, he joined Scotty in the men's room.

A short time after they pulled out of the rest station, Kurt glanced in the rear-view mirror and saw that the Mercedes was behind them again. He cursed silently. Now he was sure they were being followed. These weren't cops. Cops didn't ride around in new Mercedeses. Who the hell was tailing them? And why?

As they neared Vandergriff, he turned off sharply onto the back road that led past the abandoned quarry. He succeeded in losing the Mercedes, but he knew it would take whoever was following them just a short time to figure it out. For sure, they'd show up in the town.

Only then, hopefully, he would be alone. He had a few questions to ask these guys.

It was noon when they pulled into the driveway of the house. His glance swept the nearby street. There was no sign of a dark blue Mercedes.

"As soon as we change our clothes, Scotty, we're going to the bookstore," Maddie said as she unlocked the door.

"Ah, Mom, can't I stay with Kurt?"

"No, I can use—"

The words froze in her throat as she stared horrified around the room. Chairs were upturned and pillows pulled off the couch. The kitchen was in even worse shape. Cupboard doors were open, drawers were pulled out, the contents dumped on the floor.

"I want to see if my room's okay," Scotty said as he headed for the stairway.

"No, stay down here," Maddie cried. "There may be someone upstairs."

Kurt reached down and pulled the Springfield out of the ankle holster. The sudden appearance of the gun in his hand deepened Maddie's shocked expression.

He moved to the stairway and Scotty followed. "I'm coming with you."

"You heard your mother. Stay here," Kurt ordered.

The boy stopped abruptly and then backed up into the protective sanctuary of his mother's arms.

Maddie's and Beth's rooms were barely touched, but Scotty's room got the worst of it. The mattress and linens had been pulled off the bed, the closet had been thoroughly ransacked and a pile of clothing and hangers lay in the center of the floor. The radio and TV set were missing, and Kurt's pack had been opened and everything in it had been pulled out and lay scattered on the floor.

"Whoever did all this is gone now," Kurt said when he came back downstairs and joined them.

"I called the sheriff," Maddie said.

"What about my room?" Scotty asked.

"Trashed. Your television and radio are gone, too, I'm afraid."

"Can I go up now?"

"Yeah, the coast is clear."

Scotty raced up the stairs to survey the damage, and as if in a daze, Maddie began to pick up the kitchen chairs and place them around the table.

"Maddie, I know this is all devastating to you, but why don't you just leave everything as is until the police arrive?"

"And why don't you get that gun out of my sight," she snapped, and left the room.

Kurt had forgotten about the gun he held. Relieved he had not left the Springfield behind in his pack, he slipped the weapon back into the ankle holster.

A few minutes later the local sheriff came through the front door that was still standing open.

Sheriff Pyle DeWitt was no stranger to Kurt. As long as he could remember, DeWitt had been sheriff. His parents had named him after the famous World War II war correspondent, Ernie Pyle.

Now in his early fifties, DeWitt hadn't changed much in the past ten years, that is if a receding hairline, slippage of the waistline and widening of the hips wasn't much of a change. The sheriff still walked with a swagger and carried a good three hundred pounds around on his six-feet-six body.

He gave Kurt a disparaging glance. "I heard you were back

in town, Bolen. I might have known you'd bring trouble with you." He didn't offer to shake hands.

"So you're still the sheriff, DeWitt. Wisconsin's pro-advocates' best argument of the need for term limits legislation."

"You always were a smart-mouth, Bolen. I was surprised to see there's no rap sheet on you. Figured by now you'd be sitting in some prison for life."

"So you tried to check me out?"

"The minute I heard you were back in town. What in hell happened here?"

"Looks like you've got trouble, DeWitt."

"*Sheriff* DeWitt, to you, punk."

"Yeah, I remember, Sheriff Pyle DeWitt, and that rhymes with Sheriff Pile of Spit."

"You've got a short memory, Bolen. That kind of talk used to get you a free go-to-jail card."

"Nothing wrong with my memory. Do you still slap around your prisoners, DeWitt?"

"Ain't had to since you and Joey Bennett left town. You heard what happened to Joey?"

"Yeah, I heard. Afghanistan. That must have tweaked your conscience a little the way you used to treat him."

"It didn't." He ambled leisurely into the kitchen. "But someone sure trashed the hell out of this place."

"You don't say."

"Where's Maddie?"

"Upstairs."

Kurt followed him back into the living room. DeWitt walked over to the bottom of the stairway. "Maddie, it's Sheriff DeWitt," he called out, and turned back to Kurt. "You got an alibi for when this happened, Bolen?"

"I can't say. When did it happen, Sheriff?"

"You'd know the answer to that better than I do. You better have a good alibi."

Maddie and Scotty came down the stairs. "Hello, Pyle."

"You've sure got a mess here, Maddie."

"Yeah, and my television and radio's been stolen, Sheriff DeWitt," Scotty said.

"Sorry to hear that, son." He tousled Scotty's hair.

Recalling how the sheriff had always enjoyed slapping around teenagers, Kurt was surprised to hear the tenderness in the bully's voice when he spoke to Scotty.

"So when did this happen, Maddie?" DeWitt asked.

"I have no idea, Pyle. We've been in Milwaukee for the past two nights."

"What about Beth?"

"She was in Milwaukee, too. Still is. She and Adele Jennings... Oh, it's just occurred to me. Maybe you better check out Adele's house, Pyle. She and Aunt Beth won't be back until tomorrow, and whoever did this might have done the same to Adele's house."

"I'll do that. In the meantime, make out a list of the valuables that are missing."

"From what I can tell, there are none."

"What about my television and radio?" Scotty piped up.

"Sweetheart, they weren't exactly valuable."

"They were to me," Scotty declared.

"Of course they were, son," DeWitt said, rumpling Scotty's hair again.

Kurt observed the exchange. It was clear DeWitt appeared to have a warm spot in his heart for Scotty. It would fizzle fast, he figured, if the sheriff knew Scotty was his son.

"Hmm," DeWitt reflected, "based on the condition of the place and what's missing, my guess is it was probably a couple kids with too much time on their hands looking to do some damage."

"You mean vandals?" Maddie asked.

"It wasn't vandals," Kurt said.

"You confessing, Bolen?" the sheriff asked.

"Kurt was in Milwaukee with us, Pyle," Maddie interjected.

"And I don't think the motive was robbery or vandalism," Kurt added.

"And I don't remember asking your opinion, Bolen."

"Don't you think you should at least dust the place for fingerprints?"

DeWitt snorted. "You watch too much television, Bolen. We don't have a crime lab here. I'd have to send them to Madison to have it done. You figure you know something we don't, smart guy?"

"For one thing, your vandalism theory stinks. This place is only messed up—no serious damage. Vandals are destructive. If this was some kids out to vandalize, the glasses and china would be smashed, pillows slashed, blankets cut up and every four-letter word, that even you can think of, would be spray-painted on the walls."

"You'd sure as hell know that better than anybody," DeWitt said sarcastically. "So it was a robbery."

"You can rule that out, too. A thief snatches electronic equipment, jewelry, silver. Saleable items that can be fenced. They wouldn't pass up the larger TV down here for a thirteen-inch one. And if anything, they'd snatch the microwave or toaster oven before grabbing a twenty dollar radio that wouldn't bring five bucks on the black market."

DeWitt rocked back on his heels. "Since you've got all the answers, hot shot, what do you think was the motive for breaking in here?"

Kurt smirked. "*Now* you're asking for my opinion?"

"So get on with it, James Bond," DeWitt grumbled.

"I figure it was someone looking for a specific item, and went to a lot of trouble to make it look like kids vandalizing."

Scotty plopped down on one of the stairs and cradled his

chin in his hands. "So why'd they have to take my television and radio?"

"But what could we possibly have that anyone would go to that much trouble for?" Maddie asked.

"Hard to say right now," Kurt replied. "Tell me, Sheriff, did you notice any strangers in town the last couple days?"

"Can't say that I did. I'll check it out with Arnie at the motel to see if anyone suspicious checked in and out. When Beth gets back home have her see if anything of hers is missing. In the meantime, I'm heading over to check out Adele's house. 'Preciate if you'd come in tomorrow and sign a statement, Maddie."

"Yes, I will, Pyle."

As soon as DeWitt left, Kurt quickly replaced the drawers in the kitchen and Scotty's bedroom, shoved his belongings back into his pack, and then told them he had an important errand to run and would be back to help them finish with the cleanup.

As much as he hated walking out and leaving them with the mess, he still had an appointment with a dark blue Mercedes.

Chapter 8

There was no sign of the Mercedes, not that Kurt expected to see it in plain sight, but there weren't that many places in Vandergriff to conceal a parked car. Even if they took a wrong turn, they had plenty of time to get here by now. The car was here somewhere. But where?

His brain felt rattled as he tried to figure out what motive could be behind Maddie's house being trashed and them being followed back to Vandergriff. It all had to be connected. Was the man he saw stalking Scotty a pedophile as he had believed, or was the bastard part of it, too?

Frustrated, Kurt smacked the steering wheel. Good Lord! If it all was connected, he'd left Maddie and Scotty unprotected!

He turned the car around and raced back to the house. By the time he got back, Maddie and Scotty had restored it to order. Even the carpet had been vacuumed. As much as he preferred keeping his suspicions to himself until he had some answers, he had to make Maddie aware of the possible danger.

"Maddie, I'd like—"

She cut him off. "Scotty, I want you to go to your room for a short time. I have something important to discuss with Kurt."

"Ah, Mom, what am I supposed to do there? I don't have a television anymore."

"I don't know. Read or play a game. What did you do before television?"

"I wasn't born yet," he said.

"Do as you're told, Scotty. I'm in no mood for obstinacy from a nine-year-old."

She was clearly nervous and frustrated, and Kurt couldn't blame her. This whole situation had him feeling just as edgy. And he was about to drop a bigger bombshell on her.

"Tell you what, pal, I'll make a bargain with you. Do as your mother asks, and when we're through, we'll go and get you a new television set."

"A new one! Wow! I never had a new one. The one I had was Aunt Beth's old one," Scotty declared, and raced up the stairs to his room.

As soon as they heard Scotty's bedroom door close, Maddie faced off with him. "I will not abide your interference with my discipline of Scotty—especially when you resort to bribery. That's the same as telling him he's right and I'm wrong."

"Chill out, Maddie. You know as well as I the kid was going to do what you asked him to do. He was just expressing a little independence. You can't expect him to snap to attention and salute every time you issue an order. He's a growing boy, not a mindless robot."

"I've gotten along this far without your opinions on child rearing, Kurt. I want you to pack up your belongings and get out of here."

"All because I don't agree with *your* child rearing?"

"That's the least of it. I've tried to keep any form of violence out of his life, but from the time you entered it, there's been nothing but that. Guns, talk of organ harvesting, rescue squads, break-ins—"

"And you're dumping the blame on me."

"Well, you're the one walking around with a loaded gun strapped to your ankle."

"I had no place to put it."

"You told us you worked for the government. You didn't say anything about guns. And Dr. Escobar said you were part of a squad that rescued hostages. Oh, you thought I didn't pay attention to that remark, didn't you?" she accused.

"No, I saw the look on your face when it was mentioned."

"So if rescuing hostages doesn't reek of violence, what do you consider does?"

"That's what I intended to talk to you about."

"And just when did you *intend* to do that?"

"As soon as we were alone."

"All right, Kurt. We're alone. I want some answers now."

"Well, I don't have all the answers *now*. I'm just as confused about most of this as you are."

She folded her arms across her chest in that don't mess with me pose of hers. "I don't think so."

"If you'd sit down and listen, I'll try to explain. There are a lot of pieces to connect and I'm not a detective."

"Try beginning with the reason you're wearing that gun," she said as she sat down at the table. "How dare you bring a loaded weapon into this house?"

"I'm sorry about that, but I couldn't very well leave it behind."

"Why do you even have a gun?"

"I'm a federal officer."

"You mean like a marshal or some such position?"

"Not exactly."

"What does *not exactly* mean?"

Maddie was nobody's fool. Her skeptical glance told him as much. She wasn't going to settle for a half-truth.

"What kind of federal officer, Kurt?" she demanded.

"I work for the CIA."

"The CIA!"

From her shocked expression, you'd think he'd just told her he was Jeffrey Dahmer, the infamous serial killer who made Milwaukee a damn sight more famous than Schlitz beer ever did.

"I'm a member of an antiterrorist special operations squad whose main function is to go in and rescue hostâges."

"So you engage in covert activities."

Her attitude was beginning to piss him off. "Is that how you see it?"

"Exactly."

"Lady, what part of the word *anti*terrorist don't you understand?"

"No matter how you spell it, you're still engaging in killing."

"Yeah, that's right, Maddie. We're the bad guys. Like six months ago when the squad was sent to rescue an ATF agent—that's Alcohol, Tobacco and Firearms Bureau, in case your violence-prohibited home has never heard of it. The agent was being tortured by the drug cartel in Nicaragua. He'd been engaged in highly covert operations—trying to curb the flow of drugs to elementary school playgrounds.

"Trouble was we got there too late to save him. When the bastards couldn't break the agent with torture to give up the name of his contact, they poured gasoline on him while he was still alive and torched him."

Horrified, Maddie slumped down on a chair. "I don't want to hear any more."

"But that's not the end of it. In addition to the agent's death, Pete Bledsoe, a member of our unit—and one of the most decent men you could ever hope to know—was killed in the effort to rescue him. Yeah, Ms. Bennett, we covert operators sure are the bad guys all right."

"Please, Kurt, I said I don't want to hear any more."

"Of course you don't, but it's time you get your head out of the sand, lady. There's new rules to the game. Armies no longer blow a bugle and yell charge. Covert action has become the operative phrase. So welcome to the 21st century, Ms. Bennett."

"A violent game? Is that how you view life, Kurt?" she said sadly.

Kurt thought for a long moment then raised his gaze and looked squarely into her gorgeous Ava Gardner eyes brimming with the compassion that now struggled with the dictum she had lived by.

"No, Maddie, it's not a game to me. The stakes are much higher than trying to win a shiny trophy. Plain and simply, it's my job."

"And the choice you made."

"Yes, the choice was mine, as it was for Pete and that ATF agent. But as the saying goes, 'It's a dirty job, but somebody has to do it.'"

"I'm sorry, Kurt, if I appear apathetic or shallow to you. It's just that I abhor any form of violence for whatever the reason. My parents were shot and killed during the violence of a bar robbery. Joey died in the violence of war."

"And you believe you can protect Scotty by keeping him ignorant that violence of any kind exists. Maddie, it's not going to happen. There's no avoiding it. Violence is everywhere, whether it's a Wisconsin bar, an Afghanistan battlefield or simple road rage. The so-called human race is a misnomer. There's nothing humane about us anymore."

She jumped to her feet. "I can't believe that. I won't believe it."

"Then you're naive, Maddie."

"Why are you so bitter, Kurt? So jaded?"

"Baggage, baby. We all carry baggage. And it's easier to ease our conscience by writing a charity check in the name of humanity than it is to practice being humane to each other."

"If that's true, why condemn me for how I'm raising Scotty?"

"Because you're not preparing him for the world he has to enter. Right now the human race isn't ready to tack that *e* on to the end of its name. Maybe someday."

"You sound as naive as you accuse me of being."

He snorted. "I didn't say it was going to happen soon. My concern is what has happened now. So come over here, sit down and I'll brief you on our situation."

Maddie sat down and listened quietly as he filled her in on the details of the last few days.

"A pedophile!" she cried out. It seemed that was all she really heard when he told her of his suspicions. "Why didn't you tell me this sooner? Scotty could have been harmed."

"Because I thought it was an isolated incident until now. I know you want me out of here, but I want to remain until I'm certain you and Scotty are not at risk."

Maybe it had been a mistake to tell her. Her distress was evident, and until he had a few answers, ignorance might have been bliss in her case. No, what in hell was he thinking? He had no choice but to warn her. Keeping these suspicions from her would be the same as what he'd just accused her of doing to Scotty. Even the Boy Scout motto was "Be Prepared."

Maddie rose to her feet again and began to pace back and forth. "I can't believe this is all connected. Why is it happening to us?"

"Maddie, this was not a simple break-in and it was clear we were followed today. I admit it's a stretch linking the incidents with Scotty to it all. That guy could have just been a pedophile."

She spun on her heel. "*Just* a pedophile! When I think of what might have happened to Scotty…" Her voice cracked.

He went over and put his arms around her. "But it didn't, honey, so don't dwell on that. However the rest *did* happen and that's what we've got to consider. I'll get out if you insist, but I don't want to leave you and Scotty unprotected until I have some answers."

Her hands gripped his shirt front as if she were drowning and she looked up at him, the tears she was fighting to restrain misting her eyes. "No, Kurt, stay. Please stay."

Overwhelmed at the sight of her fear, he cradled her cheeks between his hands. "I'm not going to let anything happen to any of you, Maddie."

He lowered his head. His next move was as instinctive as it was inevitable. He had wanted to kiss her for days, but this time he had intended the kiss to be light, gentle. A tender gesture meant to soothe her fears and give her the assurance of his protection. But the instant he felt the softness of her lips, the taste of her, he wanted so much more. With all the willpower he could muster, he broke the kiss.

Her surprise was as evident as his own as she stared up at him. He shifted his gaze to the irresistible draw of her lips. That was a mistake. Sliding his hands to her shoulders, he drew her closer, crushing her against him. She felt good. Damn good.

For ten years Maddie had nourished her memory of the father of her son with fanciful yearnings and wishful dreams. Now under the pressure of his lips, the warmth and power of his embrace, divine sensation spiraled to the pit of her stomach in a degree of aroused passion she never suspected existed within her.

"Maddie, I want to make love to you."

The murmured groan jolted her out of the erotic emotion that had consumed her. Dear God, what had come over her!

She shoved him away, and raised a hand to her flushed cheek. "Don't *ever* do that again."

If he suspected her vulnerability, he would take command more than he had already. The thought only fortified her need to not succumb to temptation.

She squared her shoulders and faced off with him. "I won't

tolerate such action. It was reckless and irresponsible. Scotty is right upstairs and could have come down at any time."

"I'll concede that point as far as timing and place goes," he said.

"We have one issue to resolve, Kurt—Scotty's safety. Don't complicate that situation by creating a distraction to gratify your male hormones."

"A couple of kisses, Maddie, are not going to distract me as far as my son's safety is concerned. So forget that mess and let's put our heads together and try to come up with a connection here. If we take the incidents with Scotty out of the mix, my guess would have to be something related to you because of the house being trashed."

"What if that isn't the issue, and it does relate to Scotty? Maybe the man was a pedophile and is afraid you could identify him. He could have been one of the men in the car you said followed us."

"I don't think so. If he'd been trailing us since yesterday, he'd have known we didn't report it."

"That's my point. He wants to make sure you don't get the chance. Why do you consider our relationship a mess?"

He looked up surprised. "What are you talking about?"

"You used the phrase *that mess*. That can only imply you think of our relationship as a mess, too."

"Why bring that up now? I thought we were going to concentrate on the problem at hand."

She blushed. "It just crossed my mind that's all."

"We'll cross that bridge at the right time and place. Right now, let's get back to your theory about our roving pedophile following us here. He would be taking a bigger chance by following us and possibly exposing himself—excuse the pun. I could take him down much easier than he could me."

"But if he doesn't know what you're trained to do, he might not think it's that much of a risk."

"Maddie, I've had a good look at this guy twice now. He's a skinny little bastard. A man my size wouldn't need training to take him down."

"Well, I can't think of anything else that happened in the past couple days that would cause all of this. We went to a ball game, the zoo and returned home. I can assure you nothing happened before we went to Milwaukee. The trouble began with your arrival."

"If so, all I can say is that for the last couple months I've been in Milwaukee without any suspicious incident occurring. If something doesn't come to mind, I guess we'll have to sit it out and wait for the next shoe to drop."

Maddie got up. "The store! I have to go. I've been sitting it out too long as it is. I can trust you to take care of Scotty?"

"Of course, but you don't think I'm going to let you out of my sight, either, do you?"

"Kurt, I still have a business to run. I can take care of myself. Besides, it would appear that I'm not the target here. It's either you or Scotty. So I'd have better peace of mind if you concentrate on protecting my son."

"*Our* son, Maddie." Kurt stood up. "Scotty, come on down," he shouted up the stairs. "We're going to your mother's bookstore." He grinned at her. "Like it or not, sweetheart, from now on we're joined at the hip—and frankly, my dear, I can't think of a better-looking hip to be attached to. And then, when this mystery is solved, we have some unfinished business to settle between us."

Chapter 9

Several cartons of books were stacked in front of the bookstore. As Kurt carried them inside, he scanned the street for any sign of the Mercedes. Where in hell was that car? There weren't that many places in town where a new Mercedes could be concealed other than a resident's private garage. If that was the case, it would put the two men on foot.

Perhaps he was barking up the wrong tree and should be looking at that possibility instead of checking out cars. Also, it would mean the two men probably had an ally in town.

That's really a stretch, Bolen!

Despite the small size of the town, much to his surprise there was a steady dribble of customers in and out of the store throughout the afternoon. Maddie appeared to know all of them by name, which eliminated them as possible suspects.

When she refused his offer of help in restocking the bookshelves, Kurt sat down to play checkers with Scotty. Minutes passed like hours as he continued to let Scotty beat him. He felt confined and would have preferred to be outside looking around instead of sitting and waiting for the suspects to come to them. But he was determined not to leave either Maddie or Scotty alone and unprotected. Every tinkle of the bell when the door opened increased his edginess. Finally at seven o'clock Maddie locked up and Kurt convinced her to eat supper at the diner.

The dinner rush was practically over when they entered. Sheriff DeWitt was sitting at the counter drinking coffee and jawing with Gertie. There was a familiarity between the two that spoke of more than just a long acquaintance—DeWitt had to be sleeping with her, which didn't surprise Kurt. Ten years ago the bully had a reputation for hitting on a couple of the senior girls when he had the chance. Of course the man was always smart enough to make sure they were "Stoner" girls.

The sheriff finished his coffee, hoisted his huge bulk off the stool and came over to their booth.

"Hi, Sheriff DeWitt," Scotty greeted.

"How ya doing, Scotty? Staying out of trouble, boy?"

"You bet. And guess what, I beat Kurt in checkers, too."

"Well, he always was the dumbest pig in the pen," DeWitt said. His lip curled in a smirk. "Pen—jail. Get the connection, Bolen?

"'Bout that break-in, Maddie, I checked at the motel. Arnie said no strangers registered this past week. Just the regular travelin' salesmen that always stop. That is except for Bolen here—but he ain't no stranger to us, is he, Maddie?"

Kurt didn't miss the innuendo: it was too heavy-handed—even for DeWitt—to be just a casual remark. The piece of sleaze must have figured out who fathered Scotty.

"What about the Jennings house?" Kurt asked.

"Untouched."

"Well, thank you for your trouble, Pyle."

"No trouble, Maddie. Like I said, I think it was a couple

kids out for no good. Most likely from Stoneville," he added, smirking at Kurt as he swaggered away.

Kurt remained impassive. Smirks and sneers were the only two expressions DeWitt was capable of, and he wasn't going to give the bastard the satisfaction of getting a rise out of him.

"What a piece of work," Kurt grumbled, when DeWitt left the diner. "Does he give you any trouble, Maddie?"

"Not since Joey left."

She appeared uncomfortable with the question, which only heightened Kurt's curiosity. "Did he ever try to hit on you?"

"Not since I graduated. Before Joey left he warned DeWitt that if he gave me any trouble he'd wipe the streets with him when he got out of the marines."

Kurt chuckled. "That sounds like Joey."

"I do have to give credit where credit is due. DeWitt's always been good to Scotty." She hugged him to her side.

"Mom, why did Sheriff DeWitt hit you?" Scotty asked.

"He never hit me, sweetheart?"

"Kurt asked you if he did, and you said not since Uncle Joey left."

Maddie gave Kurt a disgusted glance. "Have you ever noticed, Kurt, that the smaller the species, the bigger their ears?"

"Elephants aren't small and they've got real big ears," Scotty said.

"You're right, honey," Maddie said. "I forgot about elephants."

Kurt flinched under the look she gave him again. If it were a knife, it would have bore a hole clean through his head. He realized, too late, that he should never have brought up the topic in front of Scotty. He wasn't used to being around kids, and in the future would have to watch what he said.

"What's your favorite animal, Scotty?" Kurt asked, in the hopes of cutting off any further questions on DeWitt.

"You mean at the zoo, or in real life?"

Kurt looked at Maddie and they both broke into laughter. "Real life, pal."

"That's easy. Dogs. I love dogs. You know, Kurt, they can be good buddies, too."

"Yeah, so I've heard. 'Man's best friend,' so they say. I thought you told me you never had a real buddy before. What kind of dog did you have?"

"Oh, I never had a dog. But I read a lot about them."

"So how come you don't have one?"

"Mom won't let me have one."

Kurt gave Maddie a wary look. "Why not, Maddie? A dog would be a great companion for Scotty."

"I feel as long as we're living in Aunt Beth's house, we shouldn't abuse her generosity any more than we do already."

"My impression of Beth is that she's too generous to ever consider it an imposition."

"Well, you're entitled to your opinion, Kurt," she said sharply, then turned her head away. "Have you decided what you want for dinner, munchkin?"

Great, Bolen! This was the second time in the last few minutes that he'd put his foot in his mouth. And the evening was still young.

"Well if this isn't a folksy looking group," Gertie said, handing them menus. "I thought you left town, Kurt."

"Hi, Gertie. I'm thinking about moving back."

"Really! Well, what do you know? Kurt Bolen's back to stay. No wonder Pyle was in such a bad mood. So what's the attraction, Kurt, as if I can't guess?" She glanced at Maddie, who appeared to be engrossed in the menu. "What do you think of Kurt moving back, Maddie?"

Maddie glanced up at her. "I think he'll find Vandergriff quite boring compared to Washington, D.C." She returned to reading the menu.

"Washington! So that's where you've been hiding. What are you going to do for a job if you move back here?"

Good question, Maddie reflected. Her mind had been so concentrated on how his move would affect Scotty that it hadn't occurred to her to ask Kurt. Obviously he intended to continue working for the CIA and divide his time between there and here.

"I'll figure out something," he said.

"Maddie, Pyle said your house was broken into. What a bummer."

"Yeah, Ms. Karpinski," Scotty spoke up. "My radio and TV were stolen, but Kurt said he'd buy me a new TV."

"Wow, honey, that's sure real generous of him. You're a lucky guy."

Scotty gave Kurt a big grin. "Yeah, we're buddies."

"I could sure use a buddy like that," Gertie said.

"Maybe if you ask him, Ms. Karpinski, he'd be your buddy, too."

"I'm sure he would," Maddie said without lifting her gaze off the menu.

"Oh, Kurt and I were always buddies. Weren't we, handsome?" Gertie said to Kurt, ignoring Maddie's jibe. "So what are you folks having?"

How comfortable they are with each other, Maddie thought. While she, on the other hand, was strung as tight as a guitar string as she listened to them. Gertie's reference to the past was a grim reminder of that final year in school. She couldn't remember one word she read on the menu, but there was no forgetting the painful memory of that senior year of high school. Kurt had any girl he wanted then, but had never given her a second glance. From the time he'd returned to Vandergriff she had fixated on that tormented memory—and as long as he remained in Vandergriff she would probably keep doing it.

In the past ten years, time and time again, she had relived

the night Scotty was conceived with gratitude—the end had justified the means. But if Kurt remained here, and she had to witness him with other women, that once-cherished memory would become as bitter as the rest of those other reminders of the past.

Throughout the meal that fear continued to monopolize her thoughts as she picked at her food. Occasionally, she could feel his stare, but did not look up to meet it.

Later, after kissing Scotty good-night, Maddie went downstairs and Kurt was watching an old movie on television.

"Scotty wants you to go up and say good-night to him."

"Yeah, I figured on doing that." He got up and took the stairs two at a time.

Feeling stifled, she went outside and sat down on the swing. A light breeze cooled her cheeks and she relaxed for the first time since they got back from Milwaukee.

It was hard to believe how her life had changed in the past few days. Until today she had thought it was only having the need to adjust to Kurt's return and his interference in raising Scotty. But if she were to believe Kurt's theory, there was the possibility of some kind of danger to Scotty and her.

The screen door slammed as Kurt came outside. "Maddie, what are you doing out here alone in the dark?"

"I'm not alone. There are plenty of mosquitoes to keep me company. That's why I turned off the lights."

He sat down beside her. "I'm glad you can be so flippant."

"Why not? I've had all day to think about this, and I'm beginning to believe you're batting at windmills, Don Quixote."

"After all that's happened?"

"Let's analyze just what that is, Kurt. You believe Scotty was stalked by a pedophile, yet, we can't be certain that was the case."

"The same man on two different occasions! Get real, Maddie. It made sense at the time."

"That's exactly what I'm trying to do. You don't know if

it was the same man. Maybe there was a faint resemblance between them. And why presume he was a pedophile? What's so unusual about a man using a men's room? It doesn't make him a pedophile?"

"Body language."

"So you're an expert on body language?"

"It's got me out of tight places a time or two. Besides, forget it. I told you I stopped thinking he was one. You're the one trying to talk me back into considering it again. How do you explain the blue Mercedes that played hide-and-seek with us all the way from Milwaukee? Don't try and pass that off as two different vehicles, coincidentally with two passengers."

"According to Pyle there are no strangers in town, and I can't think a new Mercedes wouldn't be noticed. I think you read more into it than was there. It was just a couple of traveling salesmen who stopped off at a customer and ended up behind us again."

"And the break-in, here?"

"Vandals, just as the sheriff suggested. Our arrival probably scared them off before they could do any more damage, so they grabbed a couple small items on general principles and took off. Pyle's theory makes more sense than that conspiracy-behind-every-tree one of yours. After all, he's been a sheriff for a long time and has been exposed to a lot of crime."

"Right! Big time! Vandergriff, Wisconsin—crime capital of the world! Screw that Sherlock Frigging Holmes! He knows squat. You're being naive, Maddie."

"Better than being as paranoid as you are."

"That's the pot calling the kettle black."

"What do you mean by that?"

"If anyone is paranoid, it's you and the way you're raising Scotty."

"Scotty is a lovable, well-adjusted child. How dare you criticize me?"

"He's too lovable. Too trusting. He's like that character Jim Carey played in a movie. Scotty's being raised in a make-believe world designed by you, the great director. What happens when you cut him loose and the big bubble bursts, Maddie? The piranhas in this world will eat him alive."

Maddie jumped to her feet. "I refuse to listen to any more of your accusations. What right have you to criticize me? Do you think you're some kind of role model he should emulate? Killing and violence is your life. If anything, *you're* one of those piranhas waiting to gobble him up."

He understood where she was coming from. Forms of violence had destroyed the family she had loved, but he still resented her considering him a thug and killer. She was prejudging him as if he were still that eighteen-year-old he'd once been.

Kurt stood up and grasped her by the shoulders. "You're right, Maddie, I'm no role model, and for sure no expert on rearing kids. I'm just trying to protect you. Both of you. And right now, despite what you think, I'm scared as hell that I'll fail, and something might happen to you and Scotty."

She shrugged out of his grasp. "May I remind you that for the past nine years Scotty and I have gotten along very well without your help. Not only weren't you in our lives, but neither were all those pedophiles, vandals and suspicious strangers that you appear to attract—or imagine. So take them with you when you leave."

She started to go back inside but he caught her arm and pulled her back into his arms. "Whether you like it or not, I'm staying. So suck it up, Maddie, and live with it."

He claimed her lips in a bruising, throbbing kiss that drained the breath from her, and she collapsed against him to keep from falling. For a long moment she gasped for a needed breath, then raised her head and looked him in the eyes.

"I told you I do not want you to kiss me, Kurt."

"But I like kissing you, Maddie. I like the feel of you in my arms."

His remark appeared to remind her that she was still clinging to him—a reminder he didn't need because his groin was very aware of the sensation of those curves pressed against him. And they felt good—damn good. She tried to step away but he held her firmly.

"Is kissing me another thing you expect me to *suck up*, like it or not?" she accused.

"Yeah, but you like it, Maddie. I can tell by your response," he said, and lowered his head.

This time, despite the testosterone surge lapping at his loins, he kept the kiss as gentle as the previous one had been fierce. When he broke it and she raised those Ava Gardner eyes, he saw that she was stunned. Confusion had replaced the anger that had gleamed in them only seconds before.

"Is this your way of punishing me?"

He cupped her cheeks between his hands and smiled tenderly at her. "I'm not trying to punish you, Maddie Bennett. I've been doing some thinking about this situation between us. Neither of us can walk away from it now because we both have Scotty's interests at heart. So I've come to a decision. For Scotty's sake, we can't make him the focus of our quarrels. Until we work out a solution to our relationship, no matter what happens, or what we say to each other in the heat of battle, we don't break down communication and go to bed at the end of the day angry with each other. That'll start rubbing off on the kid. Agreed?"

He waited for another outburst from her. Instead, after several ticks of the clock, the suggestion of a smile carried to her eyes. "Agreed, Kurt Bolen. And don't be surprised if you discover that might turn out to be a double-edged sword." She slipped out of his arms and went inside.

Her departing message perplexed him. What was behind

that mysterious Mona Lisa smile? Could it be the same smile that worked for Eve when she convinced Adam to take the first bite of that damn apple?

Bolen, get real! Vandergriff's no Garden of Eden.

Chapter 10

The next day, over Maddie's objection, Kurt and Scotty once again accompanied her to the store. While she served the weekly luncheon to the Vandergriff Women's Reading Group, the two males manned the bookstore, with the provision that the connecting door to the tearoom remain open.

Beth arrived shortly after two and they told her of the events of the past couple days.

"I can't believe it," the stunned woman said when Kurt returned to stocking the new books on the shelves. "I didn't notice any damage to the house."

"There wasn't any, Beth," Kurt said. "It was merely ransacked. We put everything back in order. Maddie thinks I'm mistaken in thinking that the events are connected."

"Well, frankly, Kurt, I can't blame her. It does seem a stretch of the imagination. According to her no one in town has seen any strangers or a blue Mercedes."

"Just the same, I think we should take some precautions.

Have you noticed any stranger following or watching you in the past few days?"

Beth shook her head. "Can't say that I have."

"And neither have I, Aunt Beth," Maddie said, joining them.

Kurt snorted. "I'm unimpressed with your powers of observation, Maddie, since you never noticed the car that followed us all the way from Milwaukee."

"So you say," Maddie said and walked away.

"Kurt, dear," Beth said, patting his arm, "I know you have Maddie and Scotty's interests at heart, but there is such a thing as coincidence."

My God, she was patronizing him! These two women were clueless!

"Just the same I'd like to be cautious for a couple days, Beth. I don't want either one of them left alone. Will you do me the favor of remaining with Maddie tomorrow while I entertain Scotty? He's been a real trouper about being holed up in this store."

"Have you told him your suspicions?"

"No. He thinks it's because of the break-in."

"Have you and Maddie told him that…" She gave him a hesitant glance. "You're his father?"

"Not yet. When this is over, we'll do it. I want to make sure we pick the right time and place."

"Time and place?" Beth smiled wisely. "Kurt, the boy adores you. He's going to be thrilled. Why are you and Maddie hesitating to tell him?"

"We have some problems to work out between us first."

"And if you don't work them out does that mean you'll leave without telling him?"

"Not a chance. He's my son and I've got a lot of years to make up for. He's part of my life now and whatever problems exist between Maddie and me cannot interfere with my being a part of his. But I want to make sure Scotty doesn't get hurt in the process."

"I have every confidence in you and my niece, Kurt. I know both of you will do the right thing."

The rest of the day passed peacefully and Kurt was relieved when they all retired for the night without any further suspicious incidents.

The following morning when Maddie and Beth prepared to leave for the bookstore, Kurt walked out to the garage with them.

"Whose bikes, Scotty?" he asked after they departed.

"Blue one's mine, the white one's my mom's, and the red one is Aunt Beth's."

Since there had been no further suspicious incidents since their return, Kurt was beginning to accept the belief of the others that whatever had happened previously had all been unrelated.

So I'm paranoid, he conceded to himself, determined to put his suspicions behind him. "How about a bike ride?"

Scotty broke into a wide grin. "Sure, but can you ride with your sore knee?"

"Good therapy," Kurt said.

"But they're girls' bikes? Won't that be hard?"

"Can't be any worse than working out on a stationary bike in the hospital. Let's give it a try."

"Which bike are you gonna ride?"

"I'll use your mom's."

A fanciful thought crossed his mind. He'd much rather be "riding Mom," but for now he'd have to settle for her bicycle.

They biked along a road that connected Vandergriff to the next town, but was now seldom used, replaced by the interstate highway.

Kurt's knee had begun to feel tight, and he welcomed the exercise despite the pain. The sooner those muscles healed, the quicker he could return to duty.

Occasionally a car passed, but traffic was few and far between. It was just as well, because it had been over fifteen years since he'd ridden a bike. After about ten miles, he began to tire and had to call a halt. He'd need a rest before attempting the ten miles back to town.

And why in hell hadn't he thought of bringing a bottle of water with him? "I think we better head back, Scotty."

"Your leg bothering you, Kurt?"

"Well, it's felt better." Kurt slipped off the bike, turned it around, and began to walk it. "Whose crazy idea was this?"

"This was fun," Scotty said. "Can we do it again sometime?"

"Sure can, pal."

"You want to rest, Kurt?"

"Wouldn't be a bad idea." Although he knew if he didn't keep moving his leg would stiffen up worse.

They halted in front of a house and a For Sale sign in the yard caught Kurt's attention. If he planned on settling down in the town, he had to start thinking of finding a place of his own. He couldn't remain at Beth's house indefinitely.

"Let's take a look around," he said.

The grass and shrubs were overgrown, but nothing a good trimming and grooming wouldn't correct. The exterior of the house looked to be in good condition. He peered through several windows and saw that the house was empty, but looked good.

Scotty's eyes brightened with excitement. "You gonna buy this house, Kurt?"

"I need a place of my own if I'm going to live here. Think I'll check it out and see what they're asking for it."

"Boy, it sure would be fun if you lived here all the time. We could go bike riding and you could teach me how to swim, and we could go to Milwaukee and see baseball games and all kinds of stuff like that. Yeah, it sure would be fun."

"You've got that right, buddy," Kurt said, with a yank to Scotty's Brewers cap.

Upon returning to town, they put away the bicycles and drove to the bank that was handling the sale of the property. The bank officer who handled the real estate was an ex-schoolmate and after renewing old acquaintances Kurt found out the asking price for the house was easily within his range. They set up an appointment for five o'clock to go through the house.

"What are we going to do now, Kurt?" Scotty asked when they left the bank.

"I'll think about it while I get my hair cut," Kurt said at the sight of a barbershop next door to the bank.

The barber greeted Scotty with a big smile when they entered. "Hi, Mr. Phillips," Scotty said.

"How do, Scotty. You here for a haircut?"

"No. Kurt is. I'm gonna watch."

"Sit yourself down right here," Phillips said, and put the cape around his neck. "So you want that buzz trimmed?" Kurt nodded. "Don't recall seeing you around. Just visiting?"

"Right now, but I used to live here. I'm thinking of moving back. Name's Kurt Bolen."

"Bolen. Sure I remember you. Especially those soap messages you and Joey Bennett used to leave on my window on Halloween. You heard about Joey, didn't you?"

"Yes."

"So what have you been up to these past years?"

"I enlisted in the navy right after graduation."

"I miss those days without you boys around. Town's pretty quiet now."

"Do you mean Kurt and my Uncle Joey were delinquents, Mr. Phillips?" Scotty asked.

"Naw, Scotty. They never hurt anybody. Just liked to kick up their heels sometimes," the old man said. "Kids today are meaner. None of them hang around town too long after they're out of school. Thanks to Sheriff DeWitt."

Within minutes Phillips finished and handed Kurt a mirror. "How's that?"

"Fine, sir."

"Kurt, can I get a haircut like yours?" Scotty asked. "Bet you never have to comb it or brush it."

"That's right. Okay, let's give it a try."

Phillips gave him a leery look. "Maybe you should ask Maddie Bennett first? She's pretty fussy about his haircuts."

"Hey, if the kid wants a buzz cut, why should she object?"

Phillips picked up the electric shaver. "Your funeral, mister."

Scotty grinned throughout the whole procedure. "Let's go and show Mom," he said, as soon as the barber finished. "Boy, wait till she sees me."

As soon as Kurt drew up in front of the bookstore, Scotty jumped out, ran ahead and burst through the door. He pulled off the Brewers cap. "Mom, look, I've got my hair cut."

Maddie turned around and stared in shock at him. Beth raised her brows. "Oh, oh!" she murmured softly.

"It's just like Kurt's," Scotty said, excitedly.

"Yes, I can see that," Maddie replied, trying to restrain her anger as she glared at Kurt.

"What?" he asked when he saw her expression.

"Kurt, may I speak to you privately?" She walked into the stockroom.

He glanced at Beth, who gave him a sympathetic smile, and then he followed Maddie.

"Close the door, please." She looked like a wound-up spring ready to pop. "How dare you have Scotty's hair cut without asking me."

"*Asking* you!"

"That's right. I'm very particular about his haircuts."

"So old man Phillips warned me."

"So why didn't you heed the warning?"

"Because Scotty wanted a haircut like mine. Don't tell me

you don't even allow the kid to get a hair cut he likes. For God's sake, Maddie, you're smothering him. The hair will grow back. So what's the problem?"

"The problem is he looks *exactly* like you now."

"So what?"

"So why didn't you just put an ad in the newspaper announcing that you're his father?"

"I have no intention of keeping it a secret, Maddie. That's why I think we should get married right away, and put an end to the talk."

"What? Are you out of your mind? I have no intention of marrying you. I don't think I even like you, Kurt."

"I thought you wanted to consider Scotty's interests, not your own. You'd rather our son grow up being tagged as a bastard."

"Scotty's too nice to people for anyone to call him names behind his back."

"Sure, as long as he remains in this Vandergriff bubble you raised him in. But there would be no challenge to his legitimacy if we were married. We can always split up later."

"You're talking insane."

"Why, because I think you should let the kid make one choice in his life—even if it's only a haircut? No way, lady!" He opened the door and strode out.

Maddie followed him, and Scotty came running over to her.

"If you don't like my haircut, I can wear my cap until it grows back in, Mom."

"It's very short, honey."

"But that's good, Mom. Now you won't have to wash it, 'cause I'll be able to do it myself. You work so hard all the time, and that way you can rest a little."

She knelt down and hugged him tightly. "You little munchkin, that's not work. I enjoy washing your hair."

"Scotty, your mother and I have something to tell you about—"

"Kurt, wait," Maddie cried. "Not here. Not now. Please wait until I can think this out."

"Is it about the house, Mom?"

"What house?"

"The house Kurt's gonna buy."

Maddie stood up. Exasperated, she looked at Kurt. "You're buying a house here?"

"I need someplace to live, don't I?"

"I thought you lived in D.C.?"

"I'm moving here. I mentioned that to you. Scotty and I went bike riding today and I saw this vacant house. It's about ten miles from here. I've got a five o'clock appointment to meet Andy Purcell there. I was hoping you'd come with us and give me a woman's point of view on it."

"Please, Mom, come with us? Kurt told me I could have my own special room there."

"And you come, too, Beth," Kurt said. "I want your opinion as well."

Beth grinned. "Love to. I wouldn't miss this for the world."

"Great! And when we're through, I'll take you all out to dinner. Come on, pal, we'll let these ladies get back to work. We'll pick you up at four-thirty."

"I don't close…" but they were already out the door "…until five o'clock," she murmured, despondently. Maddie threw her hands up in a hopeless gesture and turned to Beth. "What am I going to do with him, Aunt Beth?"

Beth smiled and kissed her on the cheek. "Enjoy it, honey. It's great to have a man around for a change."

Despite her distress at hearing that Kurt intended to establish a permanent residence in Vandergriff, Maddie liked the house. It had been well cared for by the previous owners, who had been uprooted by the husband's transfer to Philadelphia. Kurt liked it but saw a couple of things he'd change.

While Beth and Scotty examined the bedrooms, Kurt strolled outside and joined Maddie on the wooden deck that ran the length of the rear of the house. "What do you think of the place?"

"It looks good. I assume you intend to have an inspector check it out. You never know what's between the walls."

"At least all the toilets flush. That's a good sign."

"I am curious why you need a four-bedroom, three-and-a-half bath house."

"The one downstairs is only a powder room," he said. "And it doesn't hurt to have extra bedrooms when friends come to visit. I want Scotty to have a bedroom, too."

She spun on her heel and faced him. "Scotty *has* a bedroom."

"And he'll have one here, too, Maddie. This is an issue you're going to have to accept whether we marry or not. I want him to know it's his exclusively."

"You're determined to make this as difficult as you can."

"That's not true. Look, Maddie, I'm entering his life that's been pretty well set for the past nine years. I've got enough sense to know not to shake it up. I think when we tell him I'm his father, it will be enough of an adjustment."

"I don't think we'll have to tell him. Everyone who sees the two of you together will do it for us."

"I rather he hears it from the two of us…with no hostility. Dammit, Maddie, why won't you believe that I wouldn't intentionally do anything to harm him? I just want to be a part of his life. Why do you feel so threatened by me?"

The sincerity in his eyes and voice was evident, and Maddie turned away. "I know that's your intention, Kurt, but we have different opinions of what's good for him. That's my concern."

He moved to her and put his hands on her shoulders. "Maddie, I don't want to see him hurt any more than you do, by anything we do from now on. We can't always be at odds. We've got to work out an arrangement so that we don't start pulling at him from two different directions."

"You mean like today when you got him a haircut without consulting me. Is that what you call working things out?"

"Scotty wanted that cut. It wouldn't have occurred to me if he hadn't asked for it. Why do you feel it was unreasonable not to let him have it?"

"I told you why. Now everyone knows."

"Did you ever intend to tell him the truth about his father?"

"Of course. When he's older."

"Did it occur to you, if you wait too long he might resent you for it?"

She turned in his arms and looked him in the eyes. "I'll tell you what occurred to me, Kurt—you have a dangerous job. What if he finally has a father and loses him on the next mission you go on? How would that affect him? At least up to now, he's accepted your loss. But if once he has you—and loses you—it will be traumatic, and you know it." She lowered her eyes in despair.

Kurt tipped her chin up so he could see her face. "You're too pessimistic, Maddie. None of us have a guarantee on living or dying. Do you really expect me to be able to walk away from him now? Or settle for a couple of visits a year? You're his mother—but you're Mom to him. The arrangement you're suggesting will give him a father—but not a dad. The sooner I become Dad to him, instead of Kurt, the happier I'll be, because he'll know then that he has both a mom and dad who love him."

His smile was gentle as he continued. "I'm sorry, Maddie. I wish I could do what you ask, but I need every moment I can get with him. I've got nine lost years to make up, so you're going to have to cut me some slack when I step on your toes. I can only promise you it won't be intentional. You've done a great job raising him, Maddie, but he's reached an age when he needs a male influence, too, and that's where we'll be bumping heads. Will you try to understand?"

"Apparently I have no choice, do I?"

"We both have to consider what the best *choice* will be for Scotty's welfare, not our own personal ones. So should we break the news to him now, or later?"

"I have a lot to consider right now, so let's hold off until we're certain we know what we're doing. For the time being, just keep that baseball cap on him when the two of you are in public together. Shouldn't be a problem, he slept in it last night."

Chapter 11

Unable to sleep, Maddie turned on the lamp next to her bed and reached for the book on the nightstand. After fifteen minutes she had read two paragraphs.

She was so confused and in such an emotional muddle, she didn't know if she was even capable of an intelligent decision on the whole situation.

In hindsight, why had she even considered telling Kurt the truth about Scotty? Why hadn't she let him go when he'd been prepared to leave? The answer was simple—conscience.

So now what? The newest calamity was not only the presence of Kurt in Scotty's life—but in hers as well. What should she do? He was right about them not pulling Scotty from both sides, but Kurt had to be just as willing to compromise on some issues as he expected her to do.

The simple truth, Maddie, is that the situation is not going away by fretting about it. It was time she faced the situation as an adult.

She glanced at the framed needlepoint print of the Serenity Prayer that hung on the wall. The first line, *God, grant me the serenity to accept the things I cannot change,* seemed to jump out at her. Yes, it was time she faced the wisdom that prayer called for. The reality was that she couldn't change the mind of Kurt Bolen—and she had no right to deny him contact with his son. So why keep fighting it? Furthermore, Beth was right. It *was* nice having a man around to pick up some of the responsibility of raising a son. She just wished they were on the same page about how that should be done.

With that firm resolve she felt better already and became aware that she was hungry. She'd been so upset at dinner she'd barely touched her meal. Maddie put on her robe and slippers and went downstairs to have a cup of tea and a piece of toast.

The living room was dark except for the light from the television set. She walked over and was about to turn it off when she saw the figure on the couch.

"Kurt! Why are you sitting here in the dark?"

"Came down to avoid waking Scotty."

"Watching television in the dark is bad for your eyes."

"Can't be any worse than watching a movie in a theater. I couldn't sleep so I came downstairs. Can't you sleep, either?"

"Just hungry. Sorry to have bothered you. Good night."

Maddie went into the kitchen, turned on the light and then filled a mug with water and put it in the microwave. "I don't suppose you'd like a cup of tea, too," she said when Kurt followed her into the room.

"What makes you think that?"

Maddie laughed lightly. "You don't strike me as a tea drinker nor quiche eater."

He chuckled, and she liked the sound of it. "Lady, you are so right. Although I don't mind a glass of iced tea occasionally. What are you having to eat?"

"I thought I'd have a piece of toast," she said as she reached for the loaf of bread.

"I thought you said you were hungry." He opened the refrigerator and studied the contents. "Lordy, Lordy, Lordy! What do we have here?" He pulled out a can of beer. "Beth is corrupting the refrigerator. Bless you, Aunt Beth."

Actually Maddie had bought the six pack of beer for him, but she wasn't about to admit it. "We do have a bottle of brandy if you prefer something stronger, or coffee if you prefer something hotter."

"Thank you. I'll stick with the beer."

The timer on the microwave beeped, and she popped a teabag into the boiling water. Kurt began pulling out items. By the time he finished he had sausage, cheese, lettuce, mayonnaise, pickles and a tomato lined up on the counter.

"I don't suppose there's any rye bread?" he asked.

"No, sorry."

"Well, I'll just have to make do with what we've got."

Amused, she asked, "Are you expecting company, Kurt? What do you intend to build with all that?"

"A sandwich. Want one?"

"It will probably keep me awake the rest of the night, but why not?"

"That's my girl. Just sit that trim little rear end of yours down and watch a master create."

Maddie sat down at the table and sipped the hot tea as he prepared the sandwiches, but her gaze was on him, not what he was doing.

Manhood and the military had increased his handsomeness. A khaki-colored undershirt failed to disguise the breadth and brawn of the shoulders and chest beneath it, and a pair of jeans enhanced the slim-hipped, long-legged length of him. God, he was handsome! He positively sizzled with sex appeal.

She realized with every passing moment they spent

together she was becoming more and more aware of him physically—just as that love-struck, seventeen-year-old girl had once been. Surely he must have a girlfriend back in D.C. that would be making an appearance once he got settled here in Vandergriff. For all she knew, he could even have a wife tucked away back there. He wasn't wearing a ring, but what did that mean in today's society?

She watched him get two plates out of the cabinet. He always moved smoothly and soundlessly, did everything effortlessly, while she felt like a nervous klutz whenever she felt his gaze on her.

Face it, Maddie, the two of you are opposites in everything you think and do. The only thing you have—and will ever have—in common is Scotty. Only Scotty! As if he wasn't the most important thing on earth to her! What more could she ever hope to ask for than Scotty? "Isn't that more than enough?"

"It will have to be," he said.

His comment jolted her out of her musing. She hadn't realized she'd spoken the question out loud. "I'm sorry, what did you say?"

"It's going to have to be enough," he said. "But it would taste better on rye." He put the plates down in front of her, then sat down.

"Kurt, I can't open my mouth wide enough to even take a bite of this."

"You can if you try. The first bite is always the hardest."

She laughed lightly. "Like cutting the first piece of pie," she said, and bit into the sandwich. "Mmm, very tasty, Bolen."

"Told ya. So, tell me, Maddie, what do you really think of the house?"

"I told you earlier, it's a beautiful house. But I don't understand why you'd want such a large one."

"Who knows? I may decide to get married again."

About to take another bite, she raised her head. "Again? So you've been married before. What happened?"

"The bed got a little too crowded."

"Oh, you mean—"

"I guess I'm as much to blame. I was gone a lot."

"How long were you married?"

"Six whole months."

"I see. Doesn't sound like either one of you gave it much of a try."

He laughed. "Maddie, no one can ever accuse you of not saying what's on your mind."

She swallowed the bite she'd just taken. "I'm sorry, Kurt. You're right. It was incredibly rude of me and none of my business."

"You don't have to apologize. I admit I wasn't any more ready for marriage than Shelia was. We really weren't in love. Youth, alcohol, a good-looking woman and a guy with the hots make for a dangerous combination."

"How old were you?"

"Twenty-one. She was nineteen."

"That *was* young."

"Yeah, and it seems centuries ago. What about you?"

"Me!"

"Any near misses?"

"Heaven's no! I've been too busy to think about marrying."

"Why not, Maddie? You're twenty-seven now. What about the guy you were waiting for on Poorman's Peak the night I came to town?"

She looked perplexed. "What are you talking about?"

"Forget I asked."

"No. What are you trying to say?"

"You drove in just as I was driving out that night. I figured you went there to meet him."

"Well, you were wrong. I go there often to be alone and

think. Seeing you that night in the restaurant made me think of... Well it made me think of the night you—"

"Made love to you?" he asked.

Her laugh was derisive. "By the farthest stretch of imagination, it was anything *but* making love. You were drunk, and we had sex."

"Well, in all that time there must have been—or is—a special man in your life."

"There is," she said.

"Do I know him?" Then he held up his hand. "Forget I asked. It's none of my business."

"It's very much your business. And yes, you know him."

"Now, I'm intrigued."

"I'm talking about Scotty."

"Scotty's a boy, Maddie. You need a man in your life just as much as he does."

"Why does a man think he's the solution for any problem in a woman's life, when most of the time he's the cause of the problem?"

"I disagree. Most of the time a woman is the source of a man's problem."

"Only because his brain is between his legs."

Kurt couldn't help laughing. "What I meant by my earlier remark, Maddie, is obviously you've devoted the past nine years struggling to raise Scotty."

"Kurt, that struggle was worth it."

"And isn't it about time you start considering what's good for Maddie."

"I've got what I want, so please don't try and change it."

"Aside from the obvious fact that I, too, want Scotty in my life, I owe you a lot, Maddie. I want to start paying back some of that debt."

"If you really mean that, you can start by not interfering in my raising of him. I'm not denying he needs some male influence in his life, but don't try and take control of him. I won't stand by idly and let that happen."

"As far as Scotty goes, I intend to assume the responsibility of any father. And I further intend to accept the responsibility of the debt I owe my son's mother."

"You don't *owe* his mother anything. There's no price tag on him."

"I owe you for having him, Maddie. That alone took a lot of courage on your part. And you didn't give up when you were hit with the tragedies in your life that followed at the same time."

"And why do you think I didn't? Scotty gave my life a purpose—the determination to make certain he had a better life than I had."

"Maddie, neither of us can change the past, but if we work together we sure as hell can make the future better for all three of us."

"Too idealistic, Kurt. Easier said than done."

"Well, for one thing, I can contribute financially to making it easier."

"Financially? Didn't you just admit we can't change the past? I struggled through it with Aunt Beth's help, and it's behind me. Scotty always had a roof over his head and a hot meal in his stomach. Granted, I was never in the position to overly indulge him with luxuries, but frankly, I think he's the better for it. He appreciates anything he's given."

"That's obvious, and I agree, it's an endearing trait. And speaking of that very thing, I'm taking him shopping tomorrow for the television set I promised him."

"Then I'll pay for it."

"No, you won't! He's my son, too. Will you let that sink in, so it doesn't always become an issue between us?"

"Kurt, if you're buying a house, you're going to have a lot more expenses. I'm not naive enough to believe anyone makes big money in the military."

"You've got that right, but fortunately Dave Cassidy, the leader of the squad I'm in, happens to be a genius when it comes to investments. He took over my investments and other than a car and a rental lease on a small apartment in D.C. my expenses have been very minimal."

"Well, that will soon change when you buy a house. Not that it's any of my business, but what about a divorce? I'm told alimony can be very costly."

"I don't pay alimony. At the time of the divorce all I was drawing was my navy salary, and due to Shelia's infidelity and the fact that there was no child involved, the court denied her alimony."

Well, that cleared up two questions she had wondered about. "Don't you have any contact with her at all?"

"Not anymore. In the beginning I'd send her money when she was hard up, then she quit telephoning, so I lost track of her. A few years ago I got a Christmas card from her and she wrote that she'd moved to San Francisco and married some guy who owned a couple of filling stations. She has a couple of kids now, and said she's very happy. She became a born-again Christian and asked for my forgiveness. I wrote her back, gave her my blessing, and that's it. All's well that ends well, right?"

"Is it? You sound on the bitter side."

"Maybe I am, but it's nothing to do with a busted marriage. It's just a mood I'm in right now. You'd be surprised how Scotty has helped me through it."

She chuckled lightly. "Not at all. For nine years I've been on the receiving end of the magic he weaves."

She got up and carried their plates to the sink. "I guess I should try and get some sleep. You should, too."

Kurt came over to her. "Maddie, I know you don't approve of what I do for a living, but I wish you'd think seriously about our getting married."

She almost dropped the plates. "Married! That again. I've already expressed my opinion on that idea."

He took her hand and pulled her back to the table. "Sit down and listen. The reason I think it would be wise is because as my legal wife you would qualify for spousal benefits. For instance, take the load of medical insurance off your shoulders and enable you to cut down on your working hours and spend more time with Scotty. Most importantly, it would legitimize our son in the eyes of society. Isn't that a more important reason than any of the others?"

"But marriage?" She shook her head. "I don't know, Kurt. That could be a big mistake if we can't—"

"Maddie, no one knows better than I what a mistake marriage can be. I vowed I'd never consider it again until I was out of the service."

"That's another thing I'd have to consider, Kurt. The career you've chosen advocates violence and death. How can you be part of it without it affecting you?"

"I guess you'd have to trust me."

"It's goes beyond trust. I've told you before. If you were…" She took a deep breath. "If you were killed it would be devastating to Scotty having discovered a father, only to lose him. That's why I feel it would be a mistake for you to remain here—much less marry."

"Maddie, I don't want to minimize the trauma of losing a loved one, but every day due to accidents or health children lose a parent or are even orphaned. Death has no preferences or limitations for age or gender. What if something would happen to you? Wouldn't that traumatize him, too?"

"Get real, Kurt. I don't strap on a gun and go out to try and beat the odds each day. It's a far cry to die from health or accidental causes than to volunteer to risk your life."

"Then let's dissolve organizations such as the police force, airline pilots, firemen, high-rise window washers, and, above all, the military that defends our country, because they all put their lives at risk every time they put on their uniforms and go to work. Good God, woman, crossing the street is a risk, getting behind the wheel of a car is a risk, consuming some of the food we eat or the air we breathe are risks. Maddie, you can't live in a bubble, nor keep Scotty in one to protect him. I would have thought you'd accept that since we both lost parents due to tragic deaths."

"You mean violent deaths," she countered.

He grasped her by the shoulders and as she looked up at him, she was momentarily speechless at the intensity in his eyes. She knew he was right. In her effort to be overly protective of Scotty, she had allowed herself to become afraid of facing the reality that no matter what you do, you can't change what fate has willed for you.

"So what about it, Maddie, will you marry me?"

"What would you expect from me if I did?"

"We live together."

At her gasp of shock, he said, "Husband and wife, Maddie."

"I would prefer separate rooms," she said.

"No way. Same room. Same bed. Me Tarzan, you Jane."

"Would you agree to us not having sex?"

"That would be ludicrous. I will not agree to rule out sex, nor promise not to kiss or hug you. I'm affectionate by nature. I'll settle for a big bed and promise I'll back off whenever you say no, how's that?"

"You're pretty sure of yourself, aren't you?"

"Why shouldn't I be? I know you've always put Scotty's interests ahead of your own." He ran a finger along her cheek. "But as I told you, you both need a man in your lives…for more than one reason."

She tried to step away, but he wouldn't release her. "What about Aunt Beth? It would devastate her and Scotty. He adores her."

"She's welcome to live with us. I have a big house."

"And my bookstore? I wouldn't want to give it up."

"I don't expect you to, but you can hire someone in order to cut back on your hours."

Maddie couldn't help laughing. He was so damn cocky and sure of himself. "Well, you might not be as smart as you think you are, Kurt. Are *you* sure you know what you're doing? Taking on the responsibilities of a home and family can be very costly. You might be in for a big surprise."

"That's not the issue. I think it's the right thing to do. So what do you say?"

"I have to think about it."

"It's your call."

"Fine, give me a week to think about it in case you've got any idea about rushing down to city hall first thing in the morning and applying for a license."

"A week," he agreed.

"Now will you please release me, so I can go to bed?"

He pulled her closer and his mouth covered hers in a kiss that was as coaxing as it was hungry. By the time he broke it she felt weak and very confused.

"Do you intend to keep kissing me?"

"Every chance I get whether we marry or not. *You're* the one who may be in for a big surprise, Ms. Bennett. You might end up with a life after all."

He released her, and she hurried away. Maddie paused at the top of the stairs and looked back. Kurt was standing at the foot of the stairway with a smile much too confident for what was left of her peace of mind.

We'll just see about that, Kurt Bolen. Like they say, "He who laughs last, laughs loudest."

Chapter 12

The next morning after an inspector checked out the house, Kurt made a reasonable offer on the property and within the hour the owner had faxed an acceptance. Kurt phoned Dave Cassidy, and through the wonder of technology Kurt's checking and savings accounts were transferred into newly established accounts at the Vandergriff bank.

While the electronic transfers were being made, and ownership papers on the property drawn up and filed by the bank, Kurt asked the bank officer, Wally Boyle, to check in to the amount of Maddie's remaining mortgage on the bookstore.

"I can't do that, Kurt, without Maddie's authorization."

"Wally, Maddie and I are getting married. This will be my wedding gift to her."

"But it's breaking the law. The bank could be sued."

"Maddie's not going to sue you. Besides, pal, you owe me for taking the rap when you papered the school principal's backyard."

"Old Rottingham would have kicked me off the honor roll if you hadn't," Wally said.

Kurt chuckled. "Yeah, Old Rotten Ham was a real piece of work."

Wally thought deeply for a moment, then walked away and came back with the mortgage paper. "This is between us."

Kurt paid it off, and tucked the paid-up note in his pocket. Maybe small towns weren't so bad after all.

A short time later he left the bank three hundred and fifty thousand dollars poorer, but was now a mortgage-free home-owner and had made Maddie a mortgage-free owner of a bookstore. He headed for the store to tell her the news.

An Out To Lunch sign was on the door. Kurt peeked through the window and saw Maddie moving about inside. He tapped on the door and she came over and unlocked it.

"What's wrong?" she asked.

"I have something to tell you." She stepped aside and he entered and relocked the door behind him.

"Where's Scotty?"

"I'm meeting Beth and him for lunch and wondered if you wanted to join us."

"I'm eating my lunch as I check in some inventory." When she moved away, he followed her into the stockroom.

"I just came from the bank and I'm now a homeowner."

His excitement was evident. "Congratulations, Kurt."

"How about going out tonight to celebrate? Who'd have thought Kurt Bolen would ever be a homeowner? In Vander-griff?"

Maddie sighed. "I still don't understand why you'd want to be." Then she smiled. "But it's your life, Kurt, and I'm happy for you if that's what you wanted."

"I'll have to fly to D.C. before the end of the month and pack up my apartment."

"What about the lease?"

"Earlier I called Andy—Justin Anderson—he's one of the guys on the squad. He's been bunking with me while looking for a place of his own and he's taking over the lease for me. So it all worked out good."

"That's great, Kurt." She picked up a carton of books to carry into the store.

"Here, let me do that." He took the carton from her and followed her to where she began to stack the books on the shelf.

"Gotta ask a big favor of you," he said, and pulled more of the books out of the carton and handed them to her.

As they stood side by side the fragrance of her perfume teased his nostrils and he hadn't realized how tiny she was. In the flat sandals she wore, the top of her head only cleared his chin.

She turned her head and looked up at him. "What is it?"

"I figure I can get the rooms painted and the house set up before I have to report back to duty. Would you help me pick out furniture. I don't have much, other than a couple lamps, a TV and a radio."

"And you have that big house to furnish!"

"I'm sure you'd prefer to select what you want in the house. Besides, when we get married and you move in, you'll be bringing furniture with you."

She laughed. "You proposed to me for my furniture! Apparently, you have no idea what other costs go along with getting started in a new house. Hope you have deep pockets, Bolen," she said, returning to the stockroom.

"I'm cool," he said. "Dave said I'm still in good shape after unloading the three hundred and fifty thousand dollars."

Maddie reached for several books. "I thought you said you weren't going to offer a penny over three hundred thousand for the property."

"Oh, yeah, I forgot." He reached into his pocket, pulled out an envelope and handed it to her. "I thought as long as I was in the bank, I'd take care of this."

She opened it and began to read the document with a Paid in Full stamp on it. After several lines, Maddie looked up in shock. "This is the mortgage on my bookstore."

"Yes."

"You paid off the mortgage!" she cried, astounded. Trouble was, she'd said it not in joy, but in anger.

"Honey, I couldn't see the sense of paying another ten years interest on it."

"How dare you! That's my personal business. You had no right to get involved."

"For God's sake, Maddie, as your husband I'd have to assume the debt anyway. So why are you so upset?"

"What makes you think you can pry into my personal affairs? I only said I'd think about our getting married. I hadn't *agreed* to it yet. And this proves my original fears were right. You come to town and try to take over our lives. Get out of here, Kurt. Get out of our lives."

"Just relax and we'll sit down and talk this over quietly." He started to move toward her.

"Don't come near me." When he ignored her order, she threw one of the books at him.

Kurt dodged it, and she backed up and raised another one.

"Get out of here. Do you hear me? Get out of here." This time she threw two books at him.

"Is this something you learned in an anger-management class, lady?" he yelled, dodging them. "Dammit it, Maddie, I've had enough of this." He continued to advance on her and she backed into the wall. Kurt reached her, grasped her shoulders firmly and met the fury in her eyes. "This is ridiculous. Cool down. You're getting carried away," he declared sharply.

He could feel her trembling and saw fear as well as anger in her eyes.

"Then get out of here." Her words came out in ragged breathlessness. She turned her face aside.

Fighting to control his own irritation, he cradled her cheeks between his hands and forced her to look at him. "This isn't about the bank note or my prying into your personal affairs." He slid a hand down the slim column of her neck. "It's about what we've both been thinking since I came back. Are you really afraid of this, Maddie?"

Her legs threatened to buckle as she stood mesmerized and watched the slow descent of his head. The kiss was slow and controlled as he moved his mouth over hers in an exploratory kiss that she tried to resist, until the heady sensation spiraled to the core of her womanhood and the shiver that rippled her spine became one not of anger or fear—but aroused passion.

When he broke the kiss she made an effort to put up a breathless vocal resistance if not a physical one. "That's not true, you're wrong," she managed to stammer. "Just because I don't want sex with you doesn't mean I'm afraid."

Swallowing nervously, her gaze clung to the passion that kindled his eyes, and she wondered if her own was as visible.

"No, Maddie. I'm not wrong, any more than this is." He lowered his head and reclaimed her mouth again. This time hungrily, more urgently. "Say yes, Maddie. If you can look me in the eye and tell me no, I'll get out of here."

Her heart was pounding, her pulses throbbing. She told herself this was madness—but he was right. She wanted it as much as he did. Had thought of nothing else for the past ten years. Just once more—one senseless moment again—to be in his arms, to feel him inside her. There was no right or wrong to it—there was only the *need* for it. And, whatever the consequences, dear God, she had to seize the moment.

She looked up into the passionate plea in his eyes, slipped her arms around his neck, and parted her lips.

Kurt made no attempt to hurry. His mouth and tongue toyed with hers before he trailed a path to the hollow of her ear, then back to her lips. When they undressed...when he lowered her to the floor...were fleeting impressions as her mind and body swirled and responded to sensation and touch. Discomfort was forgotten with the first fusion of their lips and the ecstatic touch and exploration that followed.

No longer burdened with restraint, Maddie abandoned herself freely to the pleasure Kurt was bringing to her. She responded with an uninhibited reciprocation, and his moan of response was as satisfying to her ears as her rapturous sigh of "Kurt" was when their bodies joined in that climatic moment of ecstasy.

As Maddie lay in the afterglow of a long-awaited fantasy, she became aware of a slight sound of movement in the background. She slowly forced her eyelids open and saw that Kurt was on his feet dressing. She lay admiring the ripple of muscle across his wide shoulders. Lord, he had a magnificent body. She thought of what had just passed between them: the strength in those arms; the warm length of his heated, tanned flesh against her own; and once again the arousing sensation of desire began to warm her.

As if sensing her stare he turned and moved to her. A hot flush swept through her when his eyes ravished her in a lingering appraisal. He saw her blush and his brow quirked in a rakish angle as he reached out a hand to help her to her feet.

"You getting up, or should I come down?"

Suddenly she felt intimidated by his hovering above her and self-conscious about her nakedness and the intimacy of the moment. Aflame with embarrassment, she sat up and groped for her clothes. She could feel his fixed stare as she quickly pulled on her clothing. Now fortified, at least by an armor of clothing, she got to her feet.

The grin that tugged at the corners of his mouth irritated her. "What?" she declared.

"I'm so glad I wasn't drunk this time. No forgetting this one."

Well, if he thought she couldn't give as well as take, he had another thought coming. She raised her chin. "Not half as much as I do. At least I didn't have to bear the inept drunken groping."

He started to chuckle. "So you enjoyed it as much as I did."

"I didn't say that. I merely said it was less discomforting than being mauled by a drunk. Thanks to you I've now been reduced to total depravity. First the front seat of a beat-up Chevrolet and now the floor of a stockroom."

"Next time you can pick the time and place, sweetheart."

"I'll be glad to. It'll be on a hunk of the ice when Hell freezes over." She spun on her heel and strode out of the room.

"Just to show you, I don't bear grudges," he said as he followed her, "I do want to thank you. I enjoyed it very much."

"Fine, as long as you're throwing money around today like a drunken sailor, just leave whatever the going price is for such service on the counter on your way out."

The comment deflated whatever good humor Kurt had managed to hold on to. He lost it!

"Dammit, Maddie! You know I'm not treating you like a prostitute. I'm trying to make up for the past hardship I've caused you, but it seems in your eyes I can't do anything right. You're the mother of my son, and I've asked you to marry me, but I have no intention of becoming your whipping boy. I'll get out of your life if that's what you really want, Maddie, but I'm not getting out of Scotty's."

Kurt slammed the door on his way out.

Scotty rushed down the stairs and grabbed her hand as soon as Maddie entered the house. "Mom! Mom! Come upstairs and see the television set Kurt bought me," he said, pulling her up behind him. "It's got a twenty-inch screen."

"My goodness, it's very nice," Maddie said.

"I can get a lot more channels than I could on my old one,

and Kurt said it will be up to you to decide which ones I can watch."

"He did, did he?"

"And look at the color. It's sure better than Aunt Beth's old one, isn't it?"

"It sure is, honey. I hope you thanked Kurt properly."

"I tried, but I don't think he liked it."

"What do you mean?" she asked.

"I was so excited, I hugged and kissed him on the cheek like I always do to you, and he kind of looked funny. For a long time he hugged me back, then he looked kind of sad, Mom, and turned away. I didn't mean to make him sad, Mom. I love him. I really do. I wish he would never go away."

Maddie put her arms around him. "Sweetheart, I'm sure you didn't upset him. Kurt's just not used to being around children, and didn't know what to say. He probably thinks you did it just because he gave you a gift. You should hug and kiss him when you see him like you do to me, just to show how much you love him."

"Really? You think he won't get mad."

"I'm sure he wouldn't, you little munchkin. Furthermore, he just bought a house here, didn't he? That doesn't sound like he plans on going away, does it?"

"No, I guess not," Scotty replied with a wide grin. "But how come he didn't want me to go with him when he went over to his house? He said I should stay here and watch television. He took his pack with him, too. Just like the night he said he was leaving." His face puckered in a worried frown. "He's coming back, isn't he, Mom?"

"I don't know. This is the first I heard about it. I'll go and ask Aunt Beth. I'm sure Kurt would have told her his plans."

"I think he's mad at me. That's why he left."

"Nonsense. He adores you. If anything, he'd be mad at me, so stop blaming yourself."

"Did you have a fight?"

"We had a disagreement."

"Over him buying me the television set? I don't want it if it's gonna cause trouble between you. I love you two guys too much."

"And we two guys love you, so stop worrying. Promise?"

"Okay," Scotty said hesitantly.

"That's my boy!" Maddie hugged and kissed him, then left the room and hurried down to the kitchen. "Beth, Scotty said Kurt took his pack with him when he left."

She nodded. "He said he appreciated our hospitality and wouldn't impose upon us any longer."

"Impose? Where did he get that idea?"

"Those were *his* words, honey. Not mine."

"What else did he say?"

"Very little. He was quiet all through lunch. Then we went shopping for the television set for Scotty, we came back here, he hooked it up, packed up his clothes and left."

"Hmm. Did he seem mad, or anything like that?"

"No, just quiet, that's all. Dinner will be ready in a half hour if you want to freshen up."

As she climbed the stairs Maddie felt as if she'd just suffered an irrevocable loss. She walked into her bathroom and turned on the shower, then stripped off her clothes and for a long moment stared at her face in the mirror.

This is what you wanted, isn't it? You want him out of your life. No more interference, no more sticking his nose in your business. You got along without him before—and you can do it again. And the last thing you need on earth is his kisses or him making love to you. You can get along without that, too. You don't need it. Get it in your head right now, Maddie Bennett, you don't need it! There's nothing you need from Kurt Bolen.

Then she burst into tears and stepped into the shower stall. After crying her eyes out, she finished her shower and dressed.

She barely touched her food throughout dinner.

"I never figured on entering this recipe in the state fair, but I didn't think it was that bad," the ever-observant Beth Bennett declared when they finished the dinner dishes.

"It's not your cooking, Beth. I just wasn't hungry. Do you have any plans for tonight?"

"Yeah, kick off my shoes, stretch out on the couch and watch television."

"I have some shopping to do. Do you mind watching Scotty?"

"Not at all."

"Can't I go with you?" Scotty asked.

"You know how much you hate it when you have to wait while I try on clothes, honey. Besides, this is one of your favorite television nights. You don't want to miss it, you little rug rat." Maddie grabbed her purse, and gave Scotty a kiss on the cheek. "You be good, sweetheart, and listen to your Aunt Beth."

"Yes, Mom," he said, racing up the stairs to get back to his television.

"I won't be too late," Maddie said, and hurried out the door before Beth could ask her any questions.

Beth followed her to the door. "Take your time, dear. I'm going to bed as soon as Scotty does. And, Maddie, tell Kurt I missed him at supper."

Maddie stopped in her tracks and looked back. "Who said I'm going to…"

But Beth had already closed the door.

Chapter 13

To ease her conscience Maddie made a perfunctory stop at the dress shop to honor her excuse to Scotty for not bringing him along. Clearly she hadn't fooled Beth. Was she that obvious to everyone except the devoted son who trusted her?

Gertie Karpinski was deeply engrossed in studying one of the mannequins. Despite the woman's promiscuity, Gertie was too nice a woman to dislike. And even though she and Gertie never traveled in the same circles, the two women had remained friendly through the years.

"So where's my boyfriend tonight?" Gertie asked.

Maddie was uncertain if she meant Scotty or Kurt. It was no secret to anyone in their class that Gertie would brush off any guy she was with whenever Kurt gave her a nod.

"You must be very proud of him, Maddie. It almost makes me yearn for motherhood every time I talk to him."

At least Gertie's remark cleared up Maddie's previous puzzlement. "Yes, Scotty's a sweetheart."

"And so is his father," Gertie said.

Get used to it, Maddie. Gertie's just the first of many more who will broach the subject.

"If you're referring to Kurt—"

"The one and only. Heard he bought a house here." When Maddie nodded, Gertie added, "You two gonna hitch up?"

"Well there's the issue of Scotty we have to settle."

"Some girls have all the luck." Gertie grinned crookedly and turned her attention back to the mannequin. "You've got good taste, Maddie. What do you think of this lingerie?"

What could she say? The delicate black chiffon bra and bikinis, topped off with a transparent, black-lace peignoir was clearly more revealing than the plain white nylon tricot bra and pants she bought for herself, or the fuzzy chenille robe that she preferred.

"Very revealing, isn't it?"

"That's the good news, honey. Bad news is that I prefer red. Now with your coloring, it would look great on you."

The lingerie was intended for one purpose: seduction. Maddie couldn't imagine herself parading around in such a revealing outfit.

"I'm afraid it's too expensive for my tastes, Gertie," she said, trying not to challenge her friend's taste.

Gertie winkled slyly. "So pass Kurt by here, and see if he's interested in buying it for you."

"Gertie, I always buy my own lingerie. And besides, I'll be honest with you, I'm too shy to wear anything that revealing."

"Time you start. Especially with the man you've got. It's the kind of thing that drives a guy up a wall. And who's going to see it but him."

Maddie shook her head in embarrassment. "I have no intention of *seducing* Kurt Bolen. He's old enough to know what he wants and, if that's what it takes to keep him happy, I'm not the type."

"You've got to trust me on this, Maddie. You let him get away once—don't make the same mistake again."

"We are not having this conversation, Gertie Karpinski!" Maddie declared. "Come on, I'll buy you a cup of coffee."

Gertie glanced at her watch. "Next time. I've got to get going. I'm late for a date. Nice seeing you."

As she started away, Gertie turned her head and cried, "Go for it, girl."

Maddie broke into laughter and cast a backward glance at the mannequin.

She hurried from the store, and as Maddie drove to Kurt's house, she thought of what she would say to him. What if he slammed the door in her face, or even worse, if he laughed at her?

She was very naive when it came to men. Her relationships with them had been few and far between in the past ten years. And Kurt was the only man she had ever been intimate with. Scotty and the bookstore had monopolized most of her time. And in truth, available males were not that plentiful in Vandergriff, which was probably why she had hung on to her schoolgirl fascination for Kurt throughout the years.

When she reached his house, Kurt's Charger was parked in the driveway. For a long moment she remained in her car and struggled with her waning courage. Should she go in or not? What would she say to him? A horrific thought crossed her mind. Good Lord, what if he wasn't alone? She'd drop dead of embarrassment if he was with another woman.

Maddie lost her nerve, and reached to turn on the ignition key. Then she slumped back. Was she just looking for an excuse?

You've got spunk and determination, Madeline Bennett, so quit letting yourself be intimidated by him. Neither of you are teenagers anymore, so start acting like an adult around him.

Fired with determination, she got out of the car. She would try to glimpse him through a window. If he had company, she'd leave without disturbing him; she could always apologize tomorrow.

The front of the house was in darkness, but there was light shining from the kitchen area at the rear. Maddie followed the walk to the backyard and stepped up on the wooden deck that stretched across the rear of the house. The sliding glass door to the kitchen was open and she peeked through the screen. Kurt was on a ladder putting a long bulb into a ceiling fixture.

"Hello," she said.

"Hi," he replied.

He didn't seem surprised to see her. "May I come in?"

"It's open," he said, and turned his attention back to screwing in the long fluorescent light. "Mind handing me that other bulb on the counter?"

Maddie entered, picked up the bulb and handed it up to him. His indifference made her feel awkward. "I'm sorry about busting in on you uninvited. I hope I didn't startle you."

"You didn't. I heard you coming."

Maddie frowned. So much for her attempt at stealth.

"Now how about handing me that cover," he said. "Be careful, it's a little heavy."

Maddie handed him up the fiberglass rectangular cover, and Kurt clipped it onto the light fixture. "That does it," he said, and climbed down. "Sit down, I can't offer you anything but beer or milk."

"Beer's fine," she said, and looked around. There was nothing to sit on but the floor—and that looked dusty to her.

"Do you mind if I go outside? It's cooler."

Kurt grabbed two cans of beer out of the refrigerator, which was the only thing in the room, and they went outside and sat down on the stoop of the deck. He popped the cans of beer and handed one to her. "Sorry I don't have a glass."

"No problem," she said.

As he took a deep draft from the can she noticed the perspiration that dotted his brow. He raised the cool can and pressed it against his temple. "Feels good. I've got a man coming out tomorrow to check out the air-conditioning.

"How did you get a refrigerator delivered so quickly?"

"An extra twenty bucks." He took another draft of the beer and turned to face her. "Okay, Maddie, so much for the small talk. What's your mind?"

"I came to apologize for this afternoon. I didn't thank you for paying off the loan, and I sounded so unappreciative. So thank you. It really will help."

"It's the least I can do."

She drew a deep breath. "And I owe you an apology about the sex—"

"No apology needed," he said, cutting off her words. "You were great."

At the sight of his grin, she could feel the heat of her blush. "I wasn't referring to *that,* Kurt. I meant our argument. I blamed you, when in truth I was upset with myself."

"Why beat yourself up for being human, Maddie? Honest answer—did you enjoy it?"

"That's beside the point. We have a serious problem to resolve, our having sex only complicated it more."

"I don't buy that. The way I see it, it makes our decision easier. Especially if you enjoyed it. If you didn't—then it complicates the situation."

"Sex isn't a solution."

He snorted. "It sure as hell relieves a whole lot of tension."

"I knew this was a mistake. Thank you for the beer." She got up to leave.

"Sit down, Maddie." It was an order, not a request. She sat down again.

"We both agreed that Scotty needs two parents, not just one. The problem lies in your acceptance of that."

"Can you blame me?" she rebuked.

"I understand where you're coming from. I'm not exactly ideal father material."

"Oh, Kurt, I don't mean to imply that. It's obvious how great you are with Scotty, and he adores you. But as I've said before, it's your lifestyle that bothers me. You're committed to a job that has a high level of violence and I'm afraid some of that will rub off on Scotty."

"How much longer do you plan on keeping the kid in a bubble?"

"You have no idea how I wish I could stop, but I can't. I don't want him to change."

"Maddie, you've done a great job up to now. But it's time you let others pick up some of that load."

"You don't think Beth hasn't been doing that? I don't know what I'd have done in the past ten years without her help."

"I can imagine how rough it was for you. You were only seventeen."

"Eighteen by the time Scotty was born. When my folks died my problems seemed insurmountable. When word came that Joey was killed, I wanted to die, too, but the thought of the new life growing within me kept me going. Then Beth came to my aid and gave me a roof over my head. After Scotty was born we worked out a babysitting arrangement that enabled me to stay in college long enough to earn an associate's degree and work part time at the quarry."

"Still on a treadmill," he said.

"I suppose you could say that, but after a few years, I got the bright idea to open a bookstore. Beth put up her house as collateral so that the bank would give me the loan. Once the store was opened, I was able to bring Scotty there with me during the day, so things began to get a lot easier."

There wasn't a trace of bitterness or self-pity in her voice as she spoke. Kurt watched the changing expressions and could visualize the spunk and fortitude of the young girl facing one crisis after another. He knew he couldn't have prevented her grief at the loss of her parents and Joey, but he felt a sense of guilt for not being around to help her raise Scotty. And just as pitiful, he couldn't even recall clearly the night Scotty was conceived.

Maddie sighed deeply. "It was touch and go for a few years, but business increased gradually, and in the last couple years things have run pretty smoothly."

"Until I showed up," he said. He felt like a heel and stood up. "Ready for another beer?"

"No thanks, I'm the designated driver," she said lightly.

Kurt popped another can, returned and sat down beside her. "What about you, Kurt? What were you up to these past ten years?"

"You've heard most of it already. I went to Milwaukee, joined the navy. A broken marriage followed and then came the opportunity to transfer into the SEALs. Oh, I was still the same swaggering smart-mouth when I went into it, but the SEALs turned my life around, Maddie. It was the hardest training I've ever gone through, but they've taught me a damn sight more than how to *kill!* I've learned more about trust, teamwork and brotherhood in the military than I could ever have learned in civilian life."

"I thought you said you were in the Central Intelligence Agency," Maddie said.

"I am now, since they approached me to join RATCOM. The rest is history. Guess you could say my last ten years were a lot easier than yours because the government was looking after me."

Maddie smiled. "I doubt it was as *easy* as you'd like me to believe, Kurt. You were risking your life to save other lives."

His long stare probed the depth of hers. "And you were nurturing a very special life—our son," he said solemnly.

For a long moment their gazes locked, then she smiled nervously. "Remind me to show you the photo album I've kept of Scotty through the years."

"I'd enjoy looking at it."

Consumed by their thoughts of the past, once again a long moment of silence developed between them, until Kurt said, "I guess we both owe a lot to others for the way they have changed the possible courses our lives might have taken. That's why we can't let this opportunity slip through our fingers, Maddie. Somebody is trying to tell us something. It never crossed my mind to return to Vandergriff in the past ten years. Then one day I climbed into my car and decided to drive to the town where I grew up. Now nine days later I've discovered I have a son, I've bought a house and I've proposed marriage to you. I'm fatalistic, Maddie, and I'm not about to shrug this off casually with a 'that's life' attitude. There's some purpose behind why I climbed into my car that day."

"Are you suggesting divine intervention?" she said.

"I don't know what it is. Maybe Satan has a hand in it for all I know. But I'm sure as hell not walking away until I have the answer. And until you can accept that, we'll always be at odds. I'd have thought you'd want an answer as much as I do, and would want to work it out together." He shook his head and grinned derisively. "One thing for certain, Maddie, you sticking your head in the sand and hoping I'll disappear just ain't gonna happen."

Her thoughts in turmoil, Maddie took a deep breath and gazed up at the starlit sky. Why now, after ten years? She had struggled with that same question from the moment their gazes had met in the diner.

She turned her head and looked at him. His probing stare was fixed on her face. "You don't give a person too many options, do you, Bolen?"

"From habit, I guess. In my line of work you have to call it as you see it and make quick decisions."

"I can see how you're obviously very successful in *your*

line of work. Well, in my line of work—called motherhood—
it's necessary to take time to determine what's best for the
child you're raising. I'll cooperate as far as Scotty's situation
is concerned, but I will not be rushed into marriage until I
can step back and decide if that *is* the best thing for Scotty.
In the meantime, I'm sure you can legally declare him your
son as far as the government is concerned, which would
qualify him for any benefits he is entitled to, as well as being
your beneficiary."

"That issue's already academic. Aren't you missing the important point I've been trying to make. Growing up daily in
a household of Dad and Mom is a damn sight better for him
than visiting Dad on weekends."

"It can't be any worse than having divorced parents, which
was your solution if it didn't work out," she declared. "That's
why we shouldn't be hasty about getting married."

"What are you afraid of, Maddie? Still concerned about the
sex?"

"Kurt, I'm not as naive as you think. I realize a man's needs—
and you're a very virile man. But it would be harmful to Scotty,
and embarrassing to me, if you had to satisfy your needs else-
where. This is a small town and rumors spread quickly."

"I told you I won't force myself on you. And I'd never put
you or Scotty in such a position. I guess this is where the issue
of honor and trust come in. Is it me you don't trust, or are you
afraid you can't trust yourself?"

She scoffed. "In your dreams, Mr. Bolen. I'm not that seventeen-year-old girl anymore."

"And I'm not that drunken eighteen-year-old boy. So get
past it, Maddie, and let's make a fresh start. There's a lot at
stake now. Even if we're not in love, we aren't repulsive to
one another. And as long as we can trust one another we
should be able to build a future for Scotty."

"I won't deny it's tempting. I am human, you know."

He chuckled. "I found that out on the floor of your stockroom."

"You do understand that such incidents would not be in play. No more stockroom floors, or front seats of cars."

"Does that rule out elevators or under Christmas trees?" he asked, grinning.

Maddie laughed lightly. "This might be the dumbest thing I've ever done, but I'll give it a try. However, for now, we'll simply announce we're engaged to be married. That will give both of us a chance to back out if we don't like the arrangement."

Kurt stood up. "Are you moving in?"

"Not for now."

He reached out a hand and pulled her to her feet. "How long do you plan on us remaining *engaged?*"

"Until we're sure we know what we're doing." The warmth and pressure of his hand on hers made her aware of how difficult the task ahead would be. She slid her hand out of his. "It's late, I better get going."

"I'm not comfortable with you driving around these back roads alone at night. I'll lock up here, drive you back and bunk with Scotty tonight. You can bring us back in the morning. I've got some errands to run and he can come along with me."

She followed him into the kitchen. "Kurt, I'm a big girl. I've driven around these roads alone for the past ten years."

"I prefer my future wife give up those habits."

"There you go again, Bolen—trying to control my life."

"That's because I've got a big investment in you."

"I intend to pay you back the money, Kurt."

"I'm referring to our son, Maddie. I think he'd be very unhappy if something happened to his mother."

"Like you wouldn't be," she declared, in the hope of forcing a concession from him. He didn't disappoint her.

"You've got that right, lady."

"Fine, if it will satisfy that male protective streak of yours, you may *follow* me home. I'll see you there."

He grabbed his pack, his car keys, turned off the kitchen light and locked up the door.

It took a quarter of a mile to catch up with her.

Beth was watching television when they arrived. She was unable to disguise her pleasure when she found out Kurt was spending the night.

"You sure you don't mind my taking advantage of your hospitality again?" he asked.

"Of course not. Why should you sleep on a hard floor when there's a perfectly good bed upstairs. And Scotty will be delighted when he wakes up and sees you."

"I appreciate it, Beth. And Maddie and I have some news that we wanted you to be the first to know. We're getting married."

"Engaged," Maddie corrected. "I'm not rushing into anything until I'm convinced it's workable."

Beth hugged and kissed her. "I'm so happy for you, honey."

"Don't get your hopes too high, Aunt Beth. Believe me, there are a lot of problems to work out."

"Of course it's workable," Beth enthused. "Congratulations, Kurt." She hugged and kissed him. "I can't wait to see Scotty's face when you tell him. Should we wake him up, now?"

"Good Lord, no!" Maddie exclaimed. "He'd be awake and asking questions the rest of the night. There's still so many issues to resolve."

"I figure by the time I get the house in shape, we'll have them all worked out," Kurt said.

Maddie gave him an exasperated glance. "That's one of the things we have to work on—your overbearing optimism."

Beth sighed with pleasure and sat down. "I'm so happy for all of you, but this house is going to seem so empty without you."

"Beth, we're hoping you'll come and live with us," Kurt

said. "I'm grateful for all you've done for Maddie, and you've always been a part of Scotty's life. I'm joining your family, not replacing you."

"I don't know what to say," Beth said. "It's a tremendous decision. Why would you want another obstacle to overcome?"

"Obstacle? You're too loved by all of us to think of yourself as an obstacle." He winked at her. "Besides, with that strong-willed niece of yours, I'll need an ally."

"I'm going to have to think about this."

"Don't tell me I've got two women I have to convince. If you want complete privacy, we'll build you a wing of your own. But it's settled, you're coming with us."

Maddie exchanged a glance with her beloved aunt. "You see what I mean, Aunt Beth. The man is a handful."

Beth nodded. "Well, honey, I guess we should sit back and enjoy it, because I suspect it's going to happen whether we have anything to say about it or not."

Kurt grabbed her in a bear hug. "I knew there's a reason why I love you."

"Well, I'm going to bed," Beth said. "I'm getting too old for all this excitement. Good night, my darlings."

Kurt looked like he just scored the winning touchdown in the Super Bowl. He turned to Maddie with a pleased smile. "That went well, didn't it?"

"Don't pop the champagne so soon, Bret Favre. The game's not over."

"Football analogies! My cup runneth over. Tell me you enjoy the Packers."

"I was born and raised in Wisconsin, wasn't I?" She turned away and headed for the stairs. "You coming to bed?"

"Dare I take that as an invitation?"

She paused at the foot of the staircase and glanced back at him. "Yeah, right," she snorted. "Give it up, Bolen. Just make sure you turn off the lights when you come upstairs."

Kurt's eyes followed the pleasing curve of her hips as she climbed the stairs.

You're a tough competitor, Maddie Bennett, but remember, I'm the quarterback.

Chapter 14

The following morning after a relatively restless night Maddie surveyed herself objectively in the mirror. She certainly wasn't a knockout like some of those Hollywood beauties, but she had managed to keep herself in fairly good shape.

Maddie leaned forward for a closer study of her face. Average. No blemishes a plus. Freckles had faded through the years. Nose was straight and not too long. Mouth wide enough and lips looked like anybody else's—other than Angelina Jolie. And she had no idea what Kurt meant by Ava Gardner eyes. Was it bad or good?

On a scale of one to ten she was about a six. A seven if Ava Gardner eyes were a plus.

She stepped back again for another overall inspection and she scoffed at herself. It may be your appearance could pass the test, but that's where it ends.

You're not a fun person. You're dull and uptight around him—prudish might better describe it. He needs someone who's fun, who can laugh and tease with him. Someone who is uninhibited when it comes to sex.

And she knew, no matter what he promised, it would come to sex if they married. And no matter what she told herself, she would be unable to reject it when it did. For even on the floor of the stockroom, it had been the most incredible thing she had ever experienced.

Kurt was no longer that groping, inebriated schoolboy in the front seat of a car. He was a man now—all man, hardened by the passage of time and baptism of battle. And after ten years of romantic dreams and yearnings, she now feared she was the most sexually inept woman he had ever met.

On a scale of one to ten, as far as sex goes, Maddie, you're a big, round zero!

When she went downstairs Beth was out in the garden watering her flowers. "Morning, dear. Looks like another hot day."

"Thank goodness for air-conditioning. Where's Kurt's car?"

"Oh, he's up and gone already. Took Scotty with him. He said he wants to finish painting the kitchen. Which reminds me, he wants to take you out to lunch and then have you help him pick out a bedroom set. He said he'd pick you up at quarter to twelve."

"I can't. I have a business to run."

"I told him I would take care of the store while you did."

"Oh, now the two of you are deciding my daily schedules."

"Relax, honey. Nobody's trying to run your life. He has a perfectly logical explanation."

She folded her arms across her chest. "And what would that be?"

"Since you'll be living in the house, he thinks you should decide what goes into it."

"It will be your house, too, Aunt Beth. And that's what we have to discuss. Let's go inside, I need a cup of coffee."

Once seated at the kitchen table, Maddie looked around at the bright, sunny room. "I've always loved this kitchen. It's such a perfect place to start a day. I'm still struggling with the thought of leaving it. How do you really feel about moving, Aunt Beth? Kurt with his usual fashion has gone ahead and made plans without talking it over with either one of us."

"Maddie, he and I had a long talk this morning. I agree that he's impulsive, but that spontaneity is part of his charm."

"Charm! He's headstrong, set in his ways and not willing to listen to compromise."

"Think of the compromises he's made already, Maddie. One day he's a free-as-the-wind bachelor, and the next day he's taken on the responsibility of a family and home."

"And didn't stop to blink in the process," Maddie said sarcastically.

"Oh, honey, I don't believe that. I found out a great deal about Kurt Bolen this morning during our talk. Like the fact that in the past ten years he's been trained to make instant decisions. Life and death decisions that not only affect him, but the other members of his squad. On top of that, he also has tremendous loyalties. I believe most wives would find that a very redeeming quality, my dear. And I think my experience as a nurse has taught me not to be easily fooled by people. There is no doubt he has all of our best interests at heart. Honey, he wants to please *all* of us. That's why he asked me my true feelings about moving in with you. He wants my happiness as much as Scotty's and yours."

"And what did you tell him, Aunt Beth?"

"That I'm looking forward to it if he's certain he wants a maiden aunt living with him." Beth smiled. "The darling told me we're the only family he has, other than the men on his team. And he figures the CIA is going to break up the team."

"I feel sorry for him, Aunt Beth, but I don't think sympathy is a motive to marry someone."

"Perhaps, Maddie, it will be a new experience—a new beginning—for all of us. And I think that will be good for all of us, too. We all need a change in our lives. I'd hate to think that holding on to a house would prevent me from being willing to try a change in my life. I'm not *that* old yet."

"You'll always be young at heart, my dear aunt. I'm the one who fights changes. They scare me."

Beth laughed lightly. "Honey, you're a young lady on the verge of getting married. I believe it's called bridal jitters. And as I told you before, if a man like Kurt had come into my life when I was younger, believe me, my dear, we wouldn't be having this conversation."

Beth stood up and carried her cup to the sink. "So you go out to lunch and help your future husband pick out a bedroom set like any other intended bride would do. And as you do, think of all the women who would like to be in that bed with him."

"Aunt Beth!" Maddie exclaimed.

"I call it as I see it, honey."

"Well, if that's what you think, are you forgetting there's a missing ingredient here called love."

Beth smiled. "You've got to learn to trust him, Maddie, and you'll be surprised how quickly love will follow on its heels. He's a very lovable guy."

"Why do I have the impression that you're a little biased where Kurt is concerned?"

"I suppose I am. I like him, Maddie. And I can't help wonder why he showed up sitting in that booth at the diner in Vandergriff after ten years. They say the Lord travels in mysterious ways."

"You're such a romantic. A beautiful romantic, Aunt Beth. Why didn't you ever marry?"

"I never met a man I wanted to marry, my dear," Beth said lightly. "I'm pretty independent, as you may have noticed. I rarely do anything that I really don't want to do. So you and

Kurt can get that foolish idea out of your head that deep down I want to remain in this house. It's not going to happen. I can hardly wait to pick out wallpaper for my new bathroom."

Maddie got up and went over and hugged her. "I love you."

"I know you do, dear. And I know Scotty does, too, and I *know* Kurt does also. Happiness is not a house, it's being with your family. And you three are my family, the same as we are to Kurt. Besides, I've already started to sketch the layout for the garden there. Now, you better get dressed if you're planning on opening the bookstore. And, ah, Maddie…wear that pale green silk dress of yours."

"To the bookstore!"

"Why not? Besides you've got a luncheon date with your future husband. It's up to you to show him how pleasing it is to sit across a table from one another, soft music in the background as you're holding hands and talking quietly, and…playing footsie under the table."

Maddie gaped in disbelief. "Aunt Beth! Wherever did you get such an idea? What was in that coffee you drank?"

"I saw it in a movie—and it worked. Didn't you tell me I'm young at heart?"

"I lied, you're a dirty old lady." She kissed Beth on the cheek and hurried up the stairway.

Promptly at a quarter to twelve Scotty rushed into the bookstore. "We're here, Mom. You ready to go to lunch?" Beth and Kurt followed him.

"Is there any reason, Simon Legree, why Beth can't join us for lunch?" Kurt asked. "Everyone takes a lunch break. Then we can bring her and Scotty back here while we go shopping."

"That's fine with me," Maddie said.

Scotty grabbed Beth's hand. "Let's go, Aunt Beth."

Rosie's Diner was packed, but they were fortunate enough to get the last booth. The air conditioner wasn't working, so the door was propped open to let in some air. The flies accepted the invitation to lunch as well.

As for soft music and talking quietly, the noise level was deafening as people tried to talk over the blaring radio. And instead of the scent of freshly cut flowers, the smell of fried onions from the kitchen permeated the air.

"Guess this rules out holding hands or footsie," Maddie said sarcastically as she waved a fly away.

"What is that supposed to mean?" Kurt asked, perplexed.

Maddie looked meaningfully at Beth. "An inside joke."

"What's going on here, a town meeting?" he asked.

"Maybe somebody's having a party," Scotty said.

Maddie snorted. "If so, the flies seem to be the only ones enjoying it."

By twelve-thirty most of the luncheon crowd had left, and they were finally able to carry on a normal conversation.

Kurt tossed the remains of his sandwich back onto his plate. "I'm getting tired of hamburgers. I could go for a nice, juicy steak. I remember a roadhouse called Richard's about fifteen miles from here. Is it still open, or did that place close up?"

"As far as I know it is," Maddie answered.

"I worked as a busboy there for a short time. The food was always delicious. How about going there for a steak and dancing tonight, Maddie?"

She quickly rejected the offer. "I have some bookwork to catch up on."

"Nonsense," Beth declared. "It will do you good to get out and enjoy an entertaining evening for a change."

Maddie arched her brows and gave her aunt a disgruntled look. "Besides, Kurt, I thought you were going to paint your bedroom later."

"Tomorrow is another day," he said. "It's too hot to paint until the air conditioner is fixed."

"What's a busboy?" Scotty asked.

"He's the one who cleans up the table after the people leave."

"Did you like being a busboy?"

"It was okay. I only worked there a couple weeks before I was fired."

"Why were you fired?" Scotty asked.

"One of the waitresses accused me of stealing the tip from the table. Truth was, she was such a lousy waitress, they didn't leave one."

"That wasn't your fault."

"I was a kid with a bad reputation from the wrong part of town, so they believed her. I may have been a little on the wild side, but I wasn't a thief. Let that be a lesson to you, Scotty. Once you get a bad reputation, you're blamed for anything that happens. Your Uncle Joey and I didn't do half the things we were accused of doing."

"What other kind of jobs did you have?"

"Well I ushered at the Rivoli for a while and…" He broke into a grin. "I remember when I was twelve I planned to be a reporter and got a job delivering the local newspaper on my bicycle. After one week of that, I figured it was stupid for me to get up before dawn to deliver papers to people who were still enjoying their sleep. The following week— after I'd done it two mornings in a downpour—convinced me I was right, and resulted in the demise of my newspaper career."

"Which job did you like the best?" Scotty asked.

"Ushering in the theatre. It had two advantages none of the other jobs offered—free movies and all the popcorn I could eat."

"I remember when you were an usher," Maddie said. "One time I was with Joey and you let us in through an exit door."

"You mean without a ticket?" Scotty asked.

"Yes. I wanted to see the movie so badly, and we didn't have any money, so Kurt let us sneak in to see it."

"No kidding. I don't even remember that," Kurt said.

"I only did it once, but I've never forgotten it. Guilty conscience, I guess."

Scotty started to giggle. "What are you laughing about, honey?"

"I was thinking about you and Kurt being kids together with my Uncle Joey. I sure wish he hadn't died."

"Yeah, me, too," Kurt said. "We had some good times together."

"I bet I would have liked him."

"I know he would have liked you, munchkin," Maddie said.

"Do you think my father would have liked me, too?"

"I can answer that," Kurt said, "because I'm—"

"I think the conversation is getting too morbid," Maddie said, cutting him off. "This is not the place for such a discussion." She meant it for Kurt, not Scotty. "Besides, it's almost one o'clock." She stood up and the others did the same.

Kurt threw some bills on the table when Gertie handed him the check. "Take care, Gertie."

"You, too, good-looking. You finish your shopping last night, Maddie?" Gertie asked.

"No," Maddie said.

"Trust me, honey."

"Goodbye, Gertie," Maddie said, grinning.

"Bye, Ms. Karpinski," Scotty called out.

"Bye, honey," Gertie said as they departed.

Kurt dropped Beth and Scotty off at the bookstore, then he and Maddie drove to a nearby furniture store in a mall off the I-90.

After looking over several selections, they found a king-size bedroom set that pleased Kurt.

"What do you think?" he asked.

"It's very nice."

"Question is do you like it?"

"I rarely get excited over bedroom sets, Kurt."

"So what color do you want in the bedroom?" he asked.

"I hadn't given it a thought."

"What's your favorite color?"

"I don't think I have one."

"Come on, Maddie, everybody has a favorite color."

"Kurt, it's your bedroom. Whatever you're comfortable with."

"It will be *our* bedroom, Maddie. Our bed. When will that register with you? I want you to be comfortable."

"It will take more than the color of paint on the wall to make me comfortable with our arrangement, Kurt."

"Then maybe I should paint it prison gray. Maddie, you do and say a lot of things that I don't like, but I don't constantly make snide remarks or sit and pout. I'm doing my best to include you here, to make you comfortable, to make this work between us. You could attempt to meet me halfway. So get rid of that attitude, lady, so that we don't have to have an argument every day about damn foolish issues that aren't worth spit in the wind."

He turned away in disgust and motioned to the nearby salesman, who was trying to appear as if he wasn't overhearing every word they were saying.

"We've decided on this set, sir. When can it be delivered?"

They drove back to Vandergriff in silence, and Kurt pulled up in front of the bookstore. Maddie sat silently for a long moment while Kurt drummed nervously on the dashboard with his fingers.

"My favorite color is green," she said suddenly. "And I would like to accent the room with a soft yellow."

He ceased his drumming. "Okay, I'm cool with that. Date still on for tonight?"

"What date?"

"Dinner and dancing at the roadhouse."

"Kurt, I haven't gone dancing in years."

"Then it should prove interesting to see which one of us gets to lead."

They both burst into laughter.

Chapter 15

"**W**ow!" Kurt exclaimed when he glanced up and saw Maddie. The skirt of the silk halter dress she wore swirled just below the knees of her tanned legs as she descended the stairway. "No wonder your favorite color is green. You look gorgeous."

"Thank you, Kurt, but this color is celadon."

"What the hell is celadon? It looks green to me."

"Celadon is a combination of green and yellow."

"Well, *excusssse* me," he said in an exaggerated imitation of vintage Steve Martin. He winked at Scotty. "Right, pal."

Beth was wearing a cat-that-swallowed-the-canary expression. "You look lovely, dear," she said.

When they all continued to stare at her, Maddie asked, "Is my slip showing or something?"

She had taken great pains with her hair and makeup, and she thought she looked pretty good, but they were making her feel self-conscious. Had she overdone it?

"You sure look pretty, Mom," Scotty said as she hugged and kissed him goodbye.

"Thank you, sweetheart."

"Maddie, we better get going. I made the reservations for seven-thirty." Kurt put his hand on the small of her back and steered her toward the door.

"And don't give Aunt Beth any trouble, munchkin."

"He's never any trouble," Beth said. "Go, and enjoy yourselves. We've rented two movies to watch on the tube, *The Elm Street Slasher* and *Your Blood and My Guts.*"

Maddie froze in her tracks and pivoted. "What?"

Beth and Scotty broke into laughter. "Just kidding," she said. "Have a good time."

Kurt took her hand and literally pulled her out the front door.

Richard's was everything Beth had mentioned to her that morning. Soft music, fresh flowers on the table, and...air-conditioning. It was Wednesday night and the music was that of the sixties and seventies, which brought out the yuppies.

"You're a pretty old-fashion guy," Maddie said as they returned to their table after dancing to an old Barry Manilow standard.

"Why do you say that?" Kurt asked.

"Barry Manilow, Bobby Darin."

"I lean more toward Sinatra and Elvis, actually. I haven't heard anyone who can touch them. Manilow's good to dance to. When I dance with a woman, I like to hold her, not have a couple feet of floor separating us."

"Well, even your taste in movies runs to old ones. Ava Gardner and John Wayne, as opposed to today's popular stars."

"You're making me sound dull, Ms. Bennett. I'm into rock, but rappers or hip-hoppers are not my bag. I like Bruce Willis. He may not wear a Stetson or ride a horse, but he's believable. And the most successful movies today are cartoons with dubbed-in voices of movie stars."

"If you don't like today's music and movies, what do you do for entertainment?" she asked.

"I take beautiful women like you out to dinner in the hope I'll get lucky afterward."

"I'm serious, Kurt. We're relative strangers, you know. Do you enjoy reading?"

"The sports page of the newspaper or a good mystery or techno thriller."

"I'd have figured you for science fiction."

"We have enough monsters right here on earth among us, without creating invasions by weird-looking aliens. So what do you do for relaxation?"

"I mostly read, but I like biographies. We're on the same page about movies. I prefer a strong actor to carry the movie—not the special effects. I don't care for today's rock music, though. It's too loud and I can't understand a word they're saying. Normally I prefer listening to music, not lyrics, so I like classical. It's good background noise at the bookstore. That and Frank…. On occasion I listen to a couple of the country singers. Fortunately Milwaukee is close enough for me to attend a few concerts, as well as stage musicals. I love stage musicals!"

He laughed. "There's something about a man breaking into a song in the middle of a conversation that really turns me off, no matter who he is."

He reached across the table and picked up her hand. "For two people intending to marry, there's something missing." He slipped a diamond ring on her finger.

Maddie stared down in astonishment at the ring. "Kurt, it's lovely." She struggled for words but all that came out of her mouth was a stupid, "You didn't have to do this."

"I know this isn't the engagement or marriage you've dreamed of, Maddie. In the best of worlds I could have spent time courting you, so we could have discovered if we have more in common than Frank Sinatra."

"We have a son in common, Kurt."

"That goes without saying, Maddie, but a lot of marriages bust up despite having children in common. You're right. We are almost strangers. We haven't had time yet to really get to know one another—those little annoyances that often aggravate human relationships.

"Neither of us can predict the future, but if we work on the present I promise that I'll do my best to be a good husband and father to you and our son. Despite what you think, Maddie, your happiness is as important to me as Scotty's."

"It is the *present* that concerns me, Kurt. I'm still frightened by your job and the danger and violence attached to it."

"There is talk of breaking up the squad, Maddie. If they do that, I'd resign from the agency."

"What would you do?"

"Probably something in security or law enforcement. I'm pretty knowledgeable in weaponry, but would be lost in the world of high tech or big business." He rose to his feet. "How about another dance? We're wasting a good song."

She was beginning to feel brainwashed; it seemed as if they had danced together for years. Their steps matched perfectly as they moved in rhythm to an old Elvis tune. She liked the feel of his arms around her. They felt good, and she could sense the latent strength of them—and that felt good, too.

She breathed in the scent of his shaving lotion when he pulled her closer, and she rested her head against his cheek. That felt even better.

"I wonder if they're right," Kurt whispered.

She raised her head and looked into the velvet warmth of his eyes. "If who's right?" she asked.

"Those wise men Elvis sang about in this song. Do you think people rush into falling in love?"

"I think we are, if they're referring to marriage," she said lightly.

"I know I did when I married Shelia. Of course, I was drunk at the time and really didn't know what I was doing."

"You indicated she cheated on you, but did you feel you loved her when you married her?"

"Sure, until I sobered up. I realized I'd made a mistake, but I figured I could grow to love her if I toughed it out."

She studied him intently. "Is that how you feel about us?"

"No. I'm cold sober and I know what I'm doing."

"I mean, do you feel we could grow to love one another?"

For a long moment, he stared at her, then he pulled her closer and she leaned her head against his cheek again. "I think we're halfway there already," he murmured softly.

Maddie felt her heart flutter, and closed her eyes. It was impossible to ignore his sensuality. The touch of his hand on her back was igniting her nerve ends, and she could feel his need in just the pressure of his fingers.

She couldn't fight that need any longer—she didn't want to—it equaled her own. They stopped dancing and halted on the floor. She raised her head to gaze up into the yearning depths of his eyes—eyes that were mirroring her own desires.

"Let's get out of here."

She nodded. Her desire for him had swelled to the point where she could no longer deny what she was feeling, any more than she could pretend she didn't know why he wanted to leave.

They didn't speak. He opened the car door for her, but didn't touch her. When she was seated, he closed the door then walked around to the driver's side, climbed in, and turned on the ignition. Still, they didn't exchange a word, but the air was so charged with tension she thought she would explode.

He drove, keeping his eyes on the road, his long fingers secure on the wheel. She wanted to reach out and cover them with her own, but she dared not, sensing he was avoiding any physical contact to hold on to his control.

Within minutes, she guessed his destination, but it seemed like an eternity before he pulled up in front of his house. Kurt shut off the ignition and walked around and opened the door, then reached out a hand and assisted her out the car.

The waiting had been intolerable, and the moment their hands made contact, he pulled her into his arms. Her senses became engulfed, spinning and twisting helplessly, as she was drawn deeper and deeper into the depths of the interminable kiss until he swept her up in his arms.

Caressing the corded column of his strong neck, she could feel the tautness that held his body in check, and slid her hand into the mahogany thickness of his hair. The crisp springiness tantalized her fingertips as she drew his head to meet her parted lips. His kiss devoured her breath.

Kurt carried her inside and lowered her to her feet. His gaze consumed her in a ravaging feast as he pulled off his jacket and tossed it aside. She kicked off her shoes and waited, trembling, as he yanked impatiently at the knot of his tie.

He returned to her and she closed her eyes, anticipating his kiss. He pressed a kiss to each of her closed lids, then reclaimed her lips again in another deep kiss. She swirled in sensation as he rained quick, moist kisses on her face and mouth.

Now, swept by a torrent of long suppressed desire, she felt his tongue lightly trace the outline of her mouth and her hunger became unbearable, her body communicating this need with a mounting, pulsating response. He nibbled at her mouth, his tongue conducting darting forays into its heated chamber. She responded with a sensuous stroke of her hand down the sinewy column of his neck into the open neckline of his shirt, and buried her fingers in the matted hair of his chest.

His hand on her hips pressed her against the intimate proof of his arousal. It excited her more. Then capturing her lips again, he released the halter of her gown and shoved it past her breasts. Shuddering with response, she gasped when his firm warm hand cupped a breast and purred sensuously when he closed his mouth around it in an exquisitely rapturous suckling. Gasping with rapture, she aborted an attempt to unbuckle his belt to press his head to her breasts instead.

Suddenly the room flooded with light, and Kurt swung around in surprise. He shoved her behind him at the sight of the two men who stood in the doorway with pointed weapons. Maddie quickly pulled up the halter of her gown to cover her breasts.

One of the men laughed, and smirked salaciously. "Don't bother, baby, we'll finish the job he started as soon as we get rid of him."

"I wish you hadn't said that," Kurt said calmly. "Now I'm going to have to hurt you."

Before either of the intruders could guess his intent, Kurt kicked the gun out of the speaker's hand, and shoved him into his accomplice. The man's shot went wild as he fell to the floor, and before he could shoot again, Kurt grabbed his arm and twisted it. The man screamed with pain as the sound of the bone cracking carried to Maddie's ears.

She watched in horror when the other man jumped on Kurt from the rear. Kurt reached back over his shoulders, grabbed the attacker around the neck, and, as if the man was a sack of feathers, he flipped him over his head and slammed him to the floor.

In the meantime, the other assailant had crawled across the floor to try and reach his fallen gun. Kurt stepped on the man's broken wrist.

"You want to tell me again what you planned to do to the woman I intend to marry?" he asked as the man writhed in pain and began to sob.

Kurt walked away and gathered up the men's guns,

dialed 911 on his cell phone and went over to Maddie. "Are you okay?"

She was too horrified to speak, and could only nod.

"Why don't you go into the powder room and fix yourself up, before the police arrive," he said, and lightly brushed some stray strands of hair off her cheek. "I'll stay here and entertain our friends."

Maddie turned like a robot and went into the powder room off the kitchen.

Kurt tucked his shirt into his pants, and straightened his tie, then he dragged the two men outside. As he suspected, there was a dark blue Mercedes parked near the foot of the driveway. He was slipping; he'd never heard the car approach the house.

In less than five minutes a squad car drove up to the house. To his disgruntlement, Sheriff DeWitt was the driver. Upon seeing Kurt, the sheriff turned off the ignition, and maneuvered his tall frame out of the car.

"Pleasure to see you again, Sheriff," Kurt said.

"I might have known if there was trouble, you'd be at the bottom of it, Bolen."

"Nothing serious, Sheriff."

"I was told there were shots fired," DeWitt said.

"Shot, Sheriff. Not shots."

The sheriff walked over to the two men on the ground. "So who are these two? Friends of yours?"

"Not really—more like yours. They had great expectations of killing me."

"That's a lie," one said. "We were lost, saw the light and stopped to ask for directions. This sonofabitch tried to kill us because we broke up him and the girl he was with."

"Is that true, Bolen?"

"Oh, right, DeWitt," Kurt said, disgusted.

"What the hell did you do to them?" The sheriff sauntered

back to his car and put in a call for an ambulance. "And where is the girl they said was with you?"

At that moment, Maddie came out of the house and joined them. "That was me, Pyle."

"So why don't you ask my fiancée, DeWitt? She witnessed the whole thing."

DeWitt nodded. "Evening, Maddie. Bolen said you can tell me what happened here."

"It all happened so quickly, I'm still shook up," she said. "Kurt and I had no sooner come in, then these two men appeared and threatened us."

"Were they in the house when you got here?"

She shrugged. "I don't know. They just seemed to appear from nowhere."

"They couldn't have been, DeWitt. I would have seen their car when I drove in."

"Am I talking to you, Bolen?" DeWitt grumbled. He turned back to Maddie. "And how exactly did they threaten you, Maddie?"

"They each were pointing guns at us?"

"She's lying, Sheriff, to cover this guy's butt," one of the men said.

"And what is your name, Mister?"

"Smith. John Smith," the man said.

"Well, shut up, Mr. Smith, till I tell you differently."

"Ain't you gonna get me some help, Sheriff?" the other assailant asked. "I'm hurting here, and you're wasting time."

"And your name?"

"Tom Jones."

"Well, Mr. Jones, I've just given your partner some advice, and I want you to follow it, too."

"I should mention, DeWitt, he's the big mouth who said he was going to bang Maddie after they got rid of me," Kurt said.

"He's lying again, Sheriff," Jones accused.

"I told all of you to shut up until you're spoken to," DeWitt said. "I'm not buying the story, Mr. Smith, that you and Mr. Jones are two little lambs who have lost their way."

"Baa, baa, baa," Kurt said.

"Now I'll ask you gentlemen one more time," DeWitt said, after a menacing glance at Kurt. "What were you doing out here?"

"Okay, we saw the house was deserted, so we figured to break in and see what we could get. Then these two showed up," Jones said. "And I'm gonna file a claim against this guy. He broke my arm and almost killed us."

"That story makes more sense than the lost sheep one did."

"Baa, baa, baa," Kurt repeated.

"This is the last warning I'm giving you. Shut your mouth, Bolen," DeWitt snapped. "You ain't out of hot water yet." He turned back to the two men. "Are you the ones who broke into the Bennett house?"

"We don't know what you're talking about," Smith said.

"Speaking of that incident, DeWitt, please take note that these two are driving a dark blue Mercedes," Kurt said. "If you recall, I told you we were followed from Milwaukee by a dark blue Mercedes. Coincidence the Bennett house was broken into, and coincidence that now my house—and I have a direct connection with the Bennett family—is the same one Smith and Jones, there, claim they only intended to rob."

"I don't need your help to remind me that fish starts to stink after three days, Bolen."

An ambulance and another squad car arrived at the scene in response to DeWitt's call. "I'll be locking these two up as soon as the medics patch them up. And I'll take those guns of theirs, Bolen. Maddie, I'll be expecting you and Bolen to come into the office tomorrow and sign a complaint."

As soon as they drove away Maddie said, "I'd like to go home, Kurt."

"Yeah, get in the car. I'll lock up." He went back inside, and saw a cell phone lying on the floor. He picked it up, and handed it to her when he climbed into the car. "Here's your cell phone, Maddie."

"That's not mine," she said.

"Then one of those idiots must have lost it. Interesting." He studied it closely, then pushed the redial key.

After several rings the phone was picked up. "Sheldon, I told you not to call me here. What do you want?" a voice asked in irritation.

Kurt recognized the speaker at once, and hung up.

There was no mistaking that cultured Hispanic accent had been that of Dr. Fernando Escobar.

Chapter 16

"You okay, Maddie?" Kurt asked, when he joined her in the car.

"Yes," she said, woodenly.

Maddie was silent on the way back to Beth's, but Kurt had a lot on his mind hashing over his suspicions about Escobar. His instincts about the man had been right, which was small consolation. But why had he pinpointed them as a target? Even more confusing, which one of them was the prime target? For some reason, he felt tonight's attack had been aimed at him, not Maddie. So what the hell for? One thing was clear in his mind: the voice on the phone had been Escobar's.

When they entered the house, Maddie went directly to the stairway. "Good night," she said.

That's when her actions hit him. Since the attack she had been unusually silent, and her pallor should have faded by now. "Maddie, wait." Kurt moved toward the stairs. "I know you've just been through a difficult experience. Do you want to talk about this? I'm sure you don't get accosted at gunpoint very often."

The look she gave him told him that the events of the past hour were the last thing she wanted to discuss. "I'm fine, really. I just need to go to bed. We can talk in the morning."

As she moved up the stairs and out of sight, he realized that one thing was for certain—he needed help. Kurt reached for his cell phone.

After the usual sundry greetings, Dave Cassidy declared, "I assume, buddy, this is important enough to call me at midnight."

Kurt glanced at the clock. "I'm sorry. But yes, it is."

"So what's the problem?"

Kurt briefed him on the events of the past few days from beginning to end.

"And you're confident that the voice on the telephone belonged to Escobar."

"Definitely. The man has a very distinctive accent."

"So what do you have in mind?"

"He does a lot of lecturing. I'm hoping there's a file on him with the dates and cities he's visited in the last few years."

"And you suspect he's involved in organ harvesting?"

"Yes, that's my suspicion. But I can't tie in why it would involve the Bennett family. Or me."

"If you were the intended target tonight, and this doctor knows you're with a special ops squad, he may be figuring that he's under suspicion by our government," Dave said.

"Maybe, whatever you find out will help to clear up the mystery. In the meantime, the two guys who tried the hit tonight are locked up in the local jail."

"I'll get back to you tomorrow," Dave said. "Watch your back, buddy."

"I can take care of myself. It's the Bennetts I'm worried about. I intend to marry Maddie Bennett."

"Congratulations, Kurt. Hope to meet her soon. I'm having

lunch with Bishop tomorrow, and I can't wait to see his expression when I tell him you're finally settling down. Ah…Kurt, how are you doing otherwise?"

"You mean about Pete?"

"Yeah."

"I'm handling it. Like the shrink said, 'it takes time.' Hear any news about the squad?"

"It doesn't look good. I'll keep you informed."

"Okay, I'll expect to hear from you tomorrow."

"Right. Again, watch your back, buddy."

"Roger, that," Kurt said, and hung up.

For a long moment he sat staring into space. His instinct said he was the target of those assailants—the Bennetts had never been. If he left them, would any threat to them leave with him or was it too late?

He made another telephone call, and when he finished, he checked all the doors and windows, then turned off the lights and went upstairs.

Beth was sitting alone at the breakfast table when Maddie came downstairs the following morning. "Good morning, dear."

After a miserable night of trying to sleep, Maddie was in no mood to attempt cheerfulness. She managed a lackluster greeting, then poured herself a cup of coffee and sat down.

"Did you enjoy your evening last night?" Beth asked.

"Didn't Kurt tell you what happened?"

"I haven't talked to Kurt this morning. He and Scotty are still in bed."

"Then you haven't heard about the fight," Maddie said.

Beth's eyes widened in surprise. "A fight? What happened?"

"Last night on the way home we stopped at Kurt's house for a moment and two men with guns attacked us."

"Good heavens!"

"They indicated that as soon as they killed Kurt they

intended to…well, apparently rape me. I don't know if they were serious, or just trying to scare us. Anyway, Kurt reacted to the threat." Maddie buried her head in her hand. "Aunt Beth, it was horrible. Kurt fought them both and got their weapons, but I've never seen anything so brutal. I remember one of them fired a shot at him."

"Oh, my God! Was he hurt?"

"No. It missed him. The fight couldn't have lasted more than a minute. He snapped the wrist of one of them as if he were snapping a dry stick. I had a feeling he would have done it to the man's neck if I hadn't been there."

"But, dear, they threatened to kill him. It was two against one and they were armed. What did you expect him to do?"

"But he would have killed them if I hadn't been there."

"You don't know that," Beth said.

"I sensed it the moment he struck out at them. What if they were telling the truth and were simply burglars?"

"If that was their intent, Maddie, why were they armed? You sound as if you're more concerned about their welfare than you are Kurt's or your own. I'll give you a 'what if'. You told me one of them fired a shot. *What if* that shot would have struck Kurt? Neither of you might be alive today."

Beth sighed deeply. "Maddie, I love you with all my heart. You've been like a daughter to me, so I've backed you in any decision you've made, but I'm going to be quite frank with you now. From the time Kurt entered the picture you've appeared to try and recognize only the worse in the man, never the good."

"That's not true, Aunt Beth. I recognize his good qualities. What frightens me is the profession he's chosen. It has to reflect some kind of violent nature within him."

"That kind of talk angers me," Beth declared. "The man saved your life last night at the risk of his own. We all should be grateful to men like Kurt."

Maddie gaped openly at her aunt. Beth had never raised her voice to her before, and they had never exchanged a cross word.

"They put their lives on the line so that others can sleep peacefully at night," Beth continued. "Others such as his own son, whom you are so fearful will grow up to be like his father. Well, in my opinion, Maddie, the best thing that could happen to Scotty is that he would grow up to emulate Kurt."

Beth took a deep breath. "I have one remaining thing to say on the subject, and then it will be a closed issue between us. Stop this cat-and-mouse game you're playing with Kurt. Do you or don't you want to marry the man? If you don't, then let him go. But don't expect him to change to fit your specifications. Life just doesn't work out that conveniently. Furthermore, he's pretty damn good just the way he is."

The last sentence came out in a sob, and Beth got up from the table and moved away to conceal her tears.

For a long moment Maddie sat in shock, unaware of the tears sliding down her cheeks, until she felt a hand on her shoulder and looked up into Beth's tear-filled eyes.

"I'm sorry, honey. I didn't mean to hurt you."

Maddie stood up and they hugged one another. "It's your life, dear, and I understand why you wouldn't be comfortable living with a man you're afraid of," Beth said. She stepped back and looked Maddie in the eyes. "Tell me the truth, honey, has he ever threatened you?"

Maddie couldn't hold back a lopsided grin. "He's threatened to remain in Vandergriff whether I like it or not."

Beth chuckled. "That *is* a pretty serious threat."

"Aunt Beth," Maddie said hesitantly, when Beth started to pick up their coffee cups.

Beth turned back to her. "What is it, dear?"

"You know what scares me the most about him? I think I'm in love with him."

Beth smiled and patted her hand. "Let me know when you're sure." Glancing at the stairway, she saw Kurt coming down the stairs with Scotty right behind him. "Here come the men in your life now.

"Good morning, boys," Beth greeted cheerfully. "I thought maybe you were planning on sleeping all day."

"I was planning to, but the snoring woke me. Worse than a barracks," Kurt said.

He walked over to Maddie. "How are you feeling today?" His gaze measured her face in an intense probe.

"I'm fine," Maddie said.

"That's good." He leaned down and kissed her lightly on the lips.

"Aunt Beth, did you see that?" Scotty exclaimed. "Kurt just kissed Mom."

"Well, buddy, now she can pass that kiss on to you. Morning, Aunt Beth," Kurt said, and kissed her cheek.

"You're pretty chipper for somebody who almost got shot last night," Beth murmured softly, so that it wouldn't carry to Scotty's ears.

"When young ears aren't around, I'd like to discuss that very thing with you," he said. At that moment his cell phone started to beep, and he pulled it out of his pocket. "Excuse me, I've been waiting for this call." He hurried from the room.

By the time he returned, the women had breakfast on the table. "Where's Scotty?"

"He went upstairs to wash his hands and get dressed while we waited for you," Maddie said.

"Well, that call was from Dave Cassidy. I called him last night to find out some information for me. He was able to come up with Dr. Escobar's speaking engagements for the past couple years."

"Dr. Escobar?" Beth asked, startled.

"I'm afraid so, Beth. I'm certain he's involved."

"Involved in what?" she asked.

"The attempt on our lives last night."

"You've got to be mistaken, Kurt. The whole thing is ludicrous. I've worked with that doctor. He's a dedicated healer. What would make you think Fernando would be associated with such men, or have any connection with what happened to you?"

"Beth, one of the men last night dropped his cell phone. I used redial. The good doctor answered the phone and addressed me as Sheldon. Which means he was using the caller ID on his phone. It's safe to assume that Smith and Jones were aliases, but now we've got a name—Sheldon. There's no sense in trying to check those guys out here, but I figure Milwaukee could help us out."

"So you're going to Milwaukee," Maddie said.

"Yeah, as soon as Andy and Don get here."

"Who are they?" Maddie asked.

"A couple…friends of mine. I called them last night. I don't want to leave any of you unprotected."

"Unprotected?" Beth said. "Aren't Smith and Jones in the hands of the police?"

"Sure, but they'll probably be arraigned today and some shyster lawyer will get them freed on bail. And until we can connect all the dots, I want to make sure you're all protected. I was hoping you'd come with me, Maddie."

"Why don't we all just go with you?" Beth said. "Wouldn't that be easier than calling in your friends?"

"I don't know how long it will take. Beth, I hope you understand that what I do, and what my friends do, is strictly confidential. It cannot go beyond this room, and above all, Scotty mustn't have any idea. Have either of you mentioned to him that I work for the CIA?"

"Of course not," Maddie said.

"That's good, because kids often let things slip unintentionally."

"Kurt, it was clear to us from the beginning that you weren't the type to be sitting behind a desk shredding paper," Beth said. "And after Fernando recognized you as one of the men who rescued those American hostages in Colombia, I knew we were right. What I can't understand is why this is happening to us, and why Fernando would be involved."

"I hope to find that out when Maddie and I go to Milwaukee."

"My first reaction was not to go," Maddie said. "But now I'm intrigued. Do you mind handling the store and Scotty again, Beth?"

"Of course not. And I agree with you, Maddie, this is about the most intriguing thing that has happened in years. And now, we're to be guarded by a couple CIA special ops members." Beth cocked a brow in amusement. "I'm thrilled."

Kurt frowned. "Aunt Beth, did I say they were CIA?"

As soon as they finished breakfast, Kurt and Maddie went to the police station to file their complaint. "You find out anything about Smith and Jones yet, DeWitt?"

"What do think this is, the FBI?"

"What about their guns? Are they licensed?"

DeWitt snorted. "John Smith and Tom Jones! Give me a break, Bolen."

"There would have to be fingerprints on the guns. Registration numbers.... Can't you check that out?"

"Sure. By the time Madison could check them out, these guys would be out on bail."

"You mean you haven't sent them to Madison yet? My God, DeWitt, it's only a couple hours' drive."

"You want to drive it, smart-mouth?"

"I've got some important business to attend to."

"Fine. You tend to yours, and let me tend to mine."

"Well, can't you at least hold them until you do?"

"On what charge? Every punk on the street has an unlicensed gun. And with only a breaking and entering charge."

Kurt exploded. "Only breaking and entering! They tried to shoot me."

"Smith said the gun went off by accident. The law says there's only so long I can hold them. They'll probably be out on bail before you get out of my office," DeWitt said.

"Then why in hell did you get us down here to sign a complaint? Come on, Maddie, let's get out of here. We're wasting our time."

"Don't go away mad, Bolen. Just go away," the sheriff called out sarcastically.

"In your face, DeWitt!"

Kurt was still fuming when they climbed back into his car. "The man borders on idiocy," he ranted, and slammed the wheel.

Maddie patted his hand. "I think he just tries to provoke you, Kurt. Pyle isn't as dumb as he acts. I wouldn't be surprised if he'd already done a couple of those things you suggested. He just likes to push your buttons."

Kurt turned his head and stared at her for a long moment. His mind had been focused on this Escobar mystery, and for the first time since it happened, he recalled how close they had come to making love last night. How she felt in his arms. How her response had set him soaring. How just her hand on his right now had shifted his testosterone into full gear.

He wanted to kiss her, but he fought the urge. With all that had happened, she would probably think he was sexually perverted.

He turned the key in the ignition and pulled out.

A heavy burden seemed to lift from his shoulders when he saw the rental car in front of the house. Reinforcements had arrived!

The sight of Don Larson and Justin Anderson was like seeing long-lost brothers. He had missed them.

"Maddie, these are a couple buddies of mine—Don Larson and Justin Anderson, who answers to the name of Andy. Gentlemen, my future bride, Madeline Bennett, who answers to the name of Maddie."

After the proper introductions were made to Beth and Scotty, Kurt took Don and Andy aside and briefed them on the situation. He knew Scotty and Beth would be safe in their hands, and an hour later, he and Maddie were on their way to Milwaukee.

Chapter 17

Upon arriving in Milwaukee, Maddie and Kurt went directly to the main library and viewed past newspapers for the dates on the Escobar list Dave had given him.

All afternoon they pursued the search and Kurt was on the verge of abandoning it when he found an article indicating that a man in the nearby city of Chicago had been a victim of organ harvesting. The date coincided with one of Escobar's speaking engagements in that city.

"But there are forty engagements on the list, Kurt, and that's the only one that matches," Maddie said when they finished. "That could be coincidence."

"We don't have access to other papers," Kurt argued. "Chicago is nearby and that's why the Milwaukee paper carried the article. And the article said that whoever had done it appeared to be an expert surgeon."

"Like Dr. Escobar is the only expert surgeon around," Maddie scoffed.

"Hey, babe, if it looks like a duck, walks like a duck, and quacks like a duck, it's a duck." He slipped an arm around her shoulder. "Come on, let's get out of here. I've got an idea. I'm going to confront Escobar eye to eye."

"I hope you don't expect him to admit anything to you," Maddie said, amused.

"The best defense is an offense. I'm going to stretch the truth a bit and I'll be able to tell a lot from the way he reacts."

"Kurt, hasn't it occurred to you that Dr. Escobar might not have had anything to do with our situation?"

"My instincts tell me otherwise." He pulled out his cell phone. "Beth gave me a number where I can reach him. If not, I'll use the redial on that phone I found."

"Shouldn't that phone be turned over to the authorities?"

"I intend to FedEx it to Mike Bishop. He'll have it in the morning. The CIA will be able to examine it and identify other calls—received or sent—from it."

"Why didn't you just give it to Pyle last night after you found it? Dropped the problem in his lap."

"Yeah, right. Like Pyle would have acted on it," he said. "Do you think I'd ever put our safety in his hands?"

"If you feel that way, you should have sent it to the FBI or CIA, or whatever, last night. This trip is an unnecessary waste of time."

"You're probably right, but I'm still going to confront the man, if I can." Kurt punched in the number Beth had given him, and after a few words, he hung up. "The good doctor has agreed to meet us."

An hour later they were seated opposite Escobar in the lobby of the convention center. "What is this urgent matter you spoke of, Mr. Bolen? I hope Beth has not taken ill."

"She's fine, Doctor. This concerns organ harvesting."

The doctor eyed him warily. "What do you mean?"

"Last night Maddie and I were attacked by two assailants

who tried to kill us. In the fight that ensued, one of them dropped his cell phone. When I used the redial on it, you answered the phone."

"I don't know what you're talking about, Mr. Bolen. And furthermore, what has that got to do with organ harvesting?"

"Drop the act, Doctor. I sent the phone to the FBI. I'm sure the government will have no problem identifying who the call was sent to, or your voice. I imagine they'll be paying you a visit soon. We're only here to find out why we've been targeted by you and your accomplices. Even Scotty appears to have been targeted. My God, man, he's a nine-year-old boy. Why is he a threat to you?"

The doctor pulled a handkerchief out of his pocket. His hand was shaking as he patted the perspiration off his brow. "So it was you on the phone last night. Believe me, I had no idea you people were at risk."

"Would you like to explain that, sir?"

Escobar sighed deeply, then looked at Kurt. "I'm relieved my involvement in it is over. I believe I spoke to you regarding a larger and better equipped hospital I am attempting to build in Colombia. The facility we have now is small, understaffed and grossly ill-equipped. Two years ago I was approached by several people who offered to help fund my aspiration if I would assist them in this organ harvesting. They are paid hundreds of thousands of dollars on the black market for organs needed by wealthy individuals who do not—or can not—wait for the needed organ to become available through proper channels.

"Jacob Waring was the first fatality I had. As wrong as it was, I had hoped to accomplish my mission, but I have failed. I've been tortured this past week knowing I am responsible for the poor man's death. I recently told my associates I want no further part of them, and in the conversation I remember I said that I had fallen under suspicion and casually mentioned your name as an example.

"I had no idea—or never suspected—they would single out any of you and threaten you, Mr. Bolen. And my deepest regret to you, Ms. Bennett. I never intended for any harm to come to you or your family."

Stricken by the doctor's confession, Maddie said, "But my son could have been harmed. Surely you can't believe the end justifies the means."

"I believe that anything that can save lives is justified, Ms. Bennett."

"It was a worthy cause, Dr. Escobar," Kurt said. "But why didn't you attempt to do it legally through volunteers?"

"Mr. Bolen, most people only volunteer for a family member or someone they care deeply about. The demand for organs far exceed the donors."

"Who are these people you've been working with, Doctor?" Kurt asked.

"It's an international organization. It will be difficult for your government to round them all up, I'm sure."

"Doctor, you have names that will help their investigation. I don't doubt if you cop a plea with the government by cooperating with them you'll be able to avoid serving jail time. You're a great surgeon, Doctor. Your skill would be wasted behind bars."

Escobar rose to his feet. "If you'll excuse me, I must leave now and 'put my house in order' as you Americans say, before I speak with your government." He hurried away.

Kurt made no effort to stop him. He had no jurisdiction over what Escobar did in Colombia, and the doctor had not confessed to doing anything more than offering his assistance in an emergency. The legality of Escobar's actions would soon be in the hands of the authorities.

When he called home Andy told him everything was quiet and there had been no further incidents other than the sheriff nosing around, asking questions. Then he called Mike Bishop and told him the results with Escobar, and got the address of where to send the cell phone. By the time that was done, darkness had descended on the city.

"How about staying in town tonight and taking in a show?" Kurt suggested. "Beth and Scotty are in good hands, and we can't do anything more than we have. At least we know now why we were the ones targeted."

Maddie was in no mood for the long car ride back, either, but insisted on separate rooms.

"Dammit, Maddie, that's ridiculous. We're both consenting adults, and you know sometime or other we're going to end up in bed together. Last night proved that."

"Last night we let ourselves get carried away. In the light of day, I'm just not ready to share a bed with you. I'm still not comfortable with the idea. Until I am, I'm not going to let a weak moment make that decision for me."

"That doesn't make any sense to me. Why continue to be coy about it?"

"I'm not being coy, Kurt. I'm just not ready. I have enough self-control not to bow to the temptation."

"Have it your way," he grumbled. "I'm sure as hell not going to force you."

They checked in at the Pfister Hotel, and even though the Escobar situation was over, Maddie was relieved when Kurt booked them connecting rooms.

The RPG exploded near by and fragments from the rocket propelled grenade shattered his knee. He fell to the ground in pain, and tried to get to his feet, but he couldn't move. The rest of the squad was yards ahead of him and he started to crawl as another RPG exploded around him.

Pete saw he was down and shouted to the others for help, but could not be heard above the sound of the gunfire and the exploding grenades. "Get out of here,"

Kurt yelled as Pete came racing back. "I'll catch up with you."

"Take it easy, mate. I'll get you out," Pete said, and hoisted him to his shoulder. As Pete started to run, a series of bullets ripped into him.

"Pete," Kurt cried out. "Pete!"

"Kurt, wake up. Wake up, Kurt."

Jolted awake, Kurt sat up and for a long moment, trembling from the effects of the recurring dream, he sat stupefied and gazed around the room.

Maddie sat down on the bedside. "It sounded as if you were having a bad dream. I heard you shouting and crying out in your sleep." She got up and went into the bathroom and came back with a damp washcloth and towel.

"Do you have nightmares often?" she asked, as she sponged the perspiration off his brow.

"Just this one," he said. "Ever since…I'm sorry I woke you. Go back to bed, Maddie."

"Who's Pete?" she asked.

He jerked up his head. "How do you—"

"You were shouting his name," she said gently before he could finish the sentence. "You've mentioned the name before."

She got up again and turned on a lamp, then rooted around in the room refrigerator until she found a tiny bottle of whiskey. After adding ice cubes to the glass, she returned to his bedside.

"Here, drink this."

"Thanks," he said. "I'm fine now. The whiskey's cleared my head." He handed her the glass.

"You want to talk about it?"

"Maddie, for the past couple of months that's all I've been talking about with the shrink at the hospital."

She put the glass down on the bed stand. "I understand."

When she got up to leave, he grabbed her hand. "Wait. Stay. Maybe you've got the answer."

"The answer to what?" she asked, and sat back down.

"Why Pete was killed, and I survived."

"I'm afraid I don't have the answer to that, Kurt. The why and when of living and dying have always been a mystery to me. I just believe it's in God's hands and you don't die if He has a purpose for you to go on living."

"So you believe Pete's purpose was to save my life."

"Apparently."

"Why? My life wasn't worth Pete dying for it."

"Apparently it was. Yours still had a purpose."

"I don't buy that, Maddie. There's no connection."

"Kurt, why did you come back to Vandergriff after ten years? Had you thought about doing it before?"

"Never crossed my mind until that morning I woke up and decided to drive back and look around at the old hometown."

"And maybe your return had a purpose you weren't aware of."

"What, for instance?"

"Meeting your son. Getting involved with Dr. Escobar. There could be a dozen reasons that we aren't aware of."

"Maddie, you rattle my brain. You bring up things that complicate my thinking."

"Not everything. I can tell by what you said earlier, you've been struggling with why your friend died and not you."

"Why shouldn't I? He died because he tried to save my life. Under the circumstances, wouldn't you feel guilty?"

"I would—but it surprises me that you do. You seem too fatalistic about life. The kind that bounces back up if you're knocked down. I'm no psychiatrist, Kurt, but I think that's how you handled your physical pain. You transferred it to a mental one of guilt over Pete's death."

"You're right, Maddie. You're no shrink. I'd say you're worse than the one I've got, if that's your theory. I figure twenty years from now my nightmare over his death will be long gone, but I'll still be hobbling around with a painful knee."

"I'd like to hear more about Pete other than he died saving your life. Was he married? Did he have children?"

Kurt hesitated, as if unwilling to go on. Then he lay back with his head on the pillow.

"No wife, no children. Pete Bledsoe and Rick Williams were Brits. They'd been members of the Dwarf Squad from the time it was created. Since it was CIA, the rules didn't apply as they do in the military, so it didn't matter they weren't Americans. They were more loyal to the squad than they were to any country."

He grinned in remembrance. "Pete's code name on the Dwarf Squad was Happy. The guy was always smiling." His grin faded to sadness. "He'd have made it out of there if he hadn't come back for me."

"Well, how did you survive after he was killed?"

"When the other guys saw we were taking fire, they came back for us, but it was too late to help Pete. He had been cut down by rifle fire when he tried to carry me out on his back."

"He must have been a very wonderful person," she said.

"Yeah, I bet you would have liked him."

"I'm sure I would have. I better get out of here and let you get back to sleep."

She leaned forward and pressed a light kiss on his lips. When she lifted her head, their gazes met. The pain from his nightmare was still visible in his eyes.

Her whole being filled with wanting to soothe the guilt for his comrade's death that continued to haunt him. And in that instant, she realized how much she loved him. How her feelings for him went far beyond a physical attraction. Her heart seemed to swell with the realization. It was a glorious feeling.

What she had considered gratefulness for fathering their son, in truth, went much deeper than mere gratitude—or any high-school crush. She had nurtured a love for this man the same as she had her son, and had never recognized it until this moment.

Driven by this new sense of urgency, she reached out and tenderly caressed his cheek. Whatever issue existed between them now seemed so petty, mindless. He was hurting from a wound as severe and scaring as the one on his knee, and she had never considered that possibility in her past condemnation of him. He was no threat to her life or Scotty's; he was a blessing.

She lowered her head and kissed him lightly on the lips, as a mother would do to her child to make the pain go away. Then she raised her head and looked into his startled eyes. His astonishment appeared to be as great as hers.

A heated stream of blood surged through her when he raised his hands to the nape of her neck, and wove his fingers into her hair. She parted her lips as he lowered her head.

The taste of whiskey was still on his lips, and as the kiss deepened, he pulled her against him. He was bare-chested, and her camisole was a thin barrier against the warmth of his flesh and slight tickle of his chest hair. She broke the kiss, drew back and pulled off the camisole. Tossing it aside, she straddled him and slipped her arms around his neck, giving him much freer access to her breasts.

Ecstatic tingles rippled her spine, and she abandoned her senses to the eroticism of his mouth and tongue on her breasts until he rolled over and flattened her on her back.

Her breath came in gasps as he trailed kisses down her stomach, pausing only to shove her bikinis past her hips and pull off his boxers. Then his hands on her thighs parted her legs as he lowered his head, and continued the descent.

When his mouth reached its intended objective she writhed in mindless rapture, calling out his name again and again as the sensation continued to build and build until she couldn't bear another minute of it—but wanted it to go on forever. She had never known—could never have imagined—such ecstasy was possible.

And then he entered her, and she experienced that inexplicable moment of the emotional and physical glory of their combined climax.

Throughout the night they lay together, examining one another's body, discovering the tender caresses and kisses of foreplay that build to an arousal, or the erotic parts of their bodies that fueled a more immediate orgasm.

Toward morning, they finally slipped into slumber.

Chapter 18

"You've been very quiet. So what's bothering you, Maddie?" Kurt asked at breakfast the following morning. "I suppose you're mad at me about last night."

"I'm not mad at you. I'm mad at myself."

"Why?"

"I'm ashamed of myself."

He shook his head in disgust. "Dammit, Maddie, we're getting married aren't we?"

"Yes."

"Then why should you be ashamed?"

"Because I enjoyed it."

Kurt grinned, and reached across the table and squeezed her hand. "And that's bad, honey?"

"Of course it is. Do you have any idea the battle I'm waging with myself?"

"Based on your response last night, I'd have to admit I don't."

"That's exactly what I mean. Everything's a joke to you.

Yes, I enjoyed it. Yes, I enjoy having sex with you. But then, in the bright light of day, I realize that doesn't change the fact that I abhor the violence you're capable of." She leaned forward with an earnest expression. "Kurt, you snapped that man's wrist as if it were a chicken bone."

"It was a chicken bone."

"What if in an outrage you'd turn that violence on me—or even worse, on Scotty?"

Kurt appeared more amused than offended. "If I haven't strangled you by now, and manage to get through this meal without doing so, you won't have to worry."

"See, there you go again. You don't take anything I say seriously."

"Of course I do. But what I'm not going to do is agonize over the fear that I'm going to harm my son or the woman I love. It ain't gonna happen, Maddie."

She continued to stare at him with a startled expression.

"What?" he asked.

"Did you just say 'the woman you love'?"

"Yeah, what about it?"

"You never told me that you loved me. Not even last night."

"Get real, Maddie. Of course I love you. I can't believe you didn't know that by now. *Especially* after last night. Are you going to eat that piece of toast?"

"No." She shoved the plate at him, and he picked up the toast and ate it.

"If you're through eating, we might as well get out of here," he said when she finished her coffee.

They left the restaurant, and once they were in the car she fastened the seat belt, folded her hands and put them in her lap.

"I know what that means," Kurt said. "What's wrong now?"

"Well, it wouldn't have hurt for you to tell me how you feel. I don't read minds, you know."

"Apparently. I don't know how many ways I could show you. I asked you to marry me, didn't I?"

"You *told* me we were getting married," she corrected.

"I bought a house to be near you, didn't I?"

"You *told* me it was to be near your son."

"Well, don't try to tell me I didn't try courting you with candlelight and wine."

"Had you thought about how much easier it would have been to simply say I love you?"

"Oh, yeah. Right. Easy for you to say."

"Exactly. It was very easy for me to say."

"Those kinds of speeches just don't run off the tongues of men, like they do with women. After all—" He suddenly stopped what he was about to say, grasped her by the shoulders and turned her to face him. "What did you say?"

"When?" she asked, with wide-eyed innocence.

"Just now."

"I said it was very easy to say."

"Say what?" he pursued.

"I love you." She lost the battle and grinned at him.

He pointed a finger at her then himself. "You mean *you* love *me*."

"You said it first," she said.

His eyes lit up like a child viewing a new-born puppy. He pulled her closer, and only the car's console between them kept him from encompassing her completely as he kissed her in a breath-robbing, heart-stopping kiss that made her feel delirious.

"Why didn't you say so last night?" he murmured, between kisses. "When I think of what we missed—"

She drew back. "You mean we actually *missed* something last night. I can hardly wait."

"Lady, you are incorrigible. Another reason why I'm head over heels in love with you."

"You mean it's not my Ava Gardner eyes you love?" she teased.

"Ava Gardner? Who's that?" He caressed her cheek tenderly and gently kissed each eyelid. "You mean Maddie's eyes."

Kurt turned the ignition on in the car and pulled away. "If you're in love with me, what was that talk at breakfast about how ashamed you feel about last night?"

"That was before you told me you loved me."

She leaned back and relaxed as Kurt drove in silence. She had never known such contentment. Her years of dreams and fantasies had come true. She had never regretted the struggle and hardship of a single mother raising a child. Sacrifice was not in her lexicon when it came to raising Scotty. She had been blessed for having him. But now, to have the love of the man whom she had always harbored in the recess of her heart was too much for her to believe. She smiled and closed her eyes.

"I think we should move up the wedding."

Kurt's sudden statement jolted her out of her drowsiness. "To when?" she asked, yawning.

"How about tomorrow?"

Her eyes popped wide open. "At least give me a couple days to prepare for it. How about Saturday?"

"You've got it, honey," he said. "But how about starting the honeymoon now?"

He took the next exit ramp off the expressway and pulled into the nearest motel.

Sheriff Pyle DeWitt stepped outside Rosie's Diner. Chewing on a toothpick, he paused and looked around. The town had rolled up its streets for the night except for a couple of the merchants. He spat out the toothpick and climbed into his squad car. He was looking forward to the end of his shift since Gertie had invited him over later to spend the night. It was a while since he'd been laid, and he wasn't going to let anything interfere with it tonight.

He rolled past the Bennett house and saw the rental car was still in the driveway. Scotty was outside on the porch with two men. He tooted his horn in passing and Scotty grinned and waved.

Beth had told him her houseguests were friends of Bolen. He snorted. "Houseguests, my foot! Those two guys have Feds stamped on their foreheads."

Suddenly, a bell went off in his brain. "I'll be damned! Bolen's one of them!" How could he have missed that before? That punk kid Kurt Bolen was a Fed!

As he continued his rounds, he saw a blue Mercedes parked in the shadows of the mall. It looked like the car belonging to those two thugs the judge had let out on bail yesterday. What the hell were they still doing in town? He'd made it clear to them he wanted them out of his town, and decided to check the plates to make sure it was the same car.

Just as he pulled up behind the Mercedes, the sheriff saw the red Charger belonging to Bolen drive past. That's all he'd need to spoil his night with Gertie if Bolen met up with Smith and Jones again. Well, there was no way he'd let that happen. Fed or not, he'd toss all three behind bars before he'd let any of them try.

The family was just moving inside when Kurt and Maddie drove up. Kurt immediately informed them of the intended nuptials on Saturday. None were more excited than Scotty to hear the news. Maddie thought he was going to burst with happiness.

She and Kurt accompanied him up to bed to tell him the biggest news of all, and once he climbed into bed, she sat down on the bedside. "Sweetheart, Kurt and I have something more to tell you," Maddie said.

Scotty looked from one to the other, his eyes glowing with

happiness waiting for what she had to say. Maddie picked up his hand and kissed it. "Scotty, do you remember I told you your daddy went away before he even knew I was going to have a baby?"

Scotty nodded and waited again for her to continue.

"Do you understand, buddy, your Dad didn't even know he had a son until he came back," Kurt added.

For the first time some of the sparkle went out of Scotty's eyes. He glanced at Maddie. "You mean he's come back, Mom?"

"Yes, he did, honey."

The boy frowned in confusion. "But if my father's come back, how can you marry Kurt now?"

Maddie struggled to get the words past the lump in her throat. "Because... Because—"

"Because I'm your father, Scotty," Kurt said.

Scotty's expression didn't change, and it was clear to both of them that their son was more confused than ever. Finally, he said, to Kurt, "Why didn't you come back sooner?"

"Your mother told you, Scotty. I didn't know I had a son."

"But why didn't you come back to my mom? Didn't you love her?"

Kurt reached for Maddie's hand. "Scotty, I love your mother more than words could ever express."

Scotty broke out into a big grin. "Really?"

"Really."

"What about you, Mom. Do you love him?"

Tears welled in her eyes as she looked at Kurt. "More than words could ever express."

"Boy, this sure is good," Scotty exclaimed. "Kurt loves Mom, Mom loves Kurt and I love both of you."

"And both of us love you," Kurt added.

Scotty crawled up on his knees and put an arm around each their necks, then he kissed each of them on the cheek. "I bet we're gonna be the best family in the whole world."

Kurt tousled his hair. "It won't be because we didn't try, buddy."

"Now I think you better get back to bed," Maddie said. "Good night, sweetheart. I love you." She leaned down and kissed him on the forehead.

"Good night, Mom. I love you, too."

"Good night, buddy. I'll be up soon. You and I are bunking together tonight."

When Kurt leaned down and kissed him on the forehead, Scotty wrapped his arms around Kurt's neck. "I love you, Dad."

Kurt hugged him tightly. "I love you, too, Son."

Maddie and Kurt joined the others, and told them of the events that had occurred in Milwaukee. Then, since Maddie was sharing Beth's bed that night, the two women went up to bed. The three men sat up for another hour hashing over old times until they all gave up and went to bed.

Don and Andy were drinking coffee in the kitchen when Kurt joined them the following morning. "Maddie will be right down. Where's Beth?"

"She went out for a walk," he said.

"Did I hear you say Beth went out for a walk," Maddie asked, joining them.

Don nodded. "She was reading the newspaper, then started crying and ran out. I went after her, but she told me she wanted to be alone."

"What was in the paper?" she asked. Don handed it to her. "Oh, dear God," she murmured, "Beth must be devastated." She handed the paper to Kurt and hurried out the door.

The picture of Escobar immediately caught his attention. The article read that Escobar's body had been found hanging in the shower stall. The police presumed it was a suicide even though there was no suicide note found. It went on to describe Escobar's distinguished career.

"Was Beth a close friend of Escobar?" Andy asked.

"I think there was nothing personal between them. Beth respected the doctor's skill as a surgeon."

"Do you think you'll be needing us anymore?" Don asked.

"No, but aren't you going to stay for the wedding?"

"Well, since the wedding isn't until Saturday, Andy and I thought we'd spend a couple days taking in Milwaukee, then come back on Saturday morning."

Beth and Maddie returned as they were leaving. Now composed, Beth warned them to behave themselves.

"We will, Aunt Beth," Andy said, as they gave her a hug and kiss on the cheek.

As soon as they left, Maddie and Beth also left to open the store. Since it appeared to be another scorcher, Kurt decided to give Scotty his first swimming lesson.

When they reached the quarry Scotty stood on the rim gazing down into the water. Kurt slipped an arm around his shoulders. "Are you afraid, Scotty?"

"Kind of." Then he nodded. "Yeah, I'm real afraid."

"There's no shame in being afraid, pal. Do you want to forget it today?"

"Will you think I'm chicken if I do?"

"No." Kurt moved over to a large boulder and sat down.

"I bet you've never been afraid of anything," Scotty said, sitting down beside him.

"Oh, yes I have. Plenty of times."

"Like when?"

"When I became a navy SEAL. I had to learn to do things in water that I didn't think I could do. So let's start with you learning how to hold your breath."

"Will you teach me?"

"Can't do it up here." He went over and dived into the water. "Come on in, Scotty. I'll be right at your side. Just take a deep breath and jump. Trust me, I won't let anything happen to you."

Scotty hesitated for a moment, then jumped into the water. Kurt brought him to the surface immediately.

Once in the water, he had Scotty close his eyes and hold his breath, then supported him under his back as the boy floated just under the water's surface.

By the time they stopped after an hour, Kurt was proud of his son. He was doing a darn sight better than when they began and more important, Scotty's trust in him prevented the boy from panicking. Kurt was beginning to really jell in his father role.

They were on the verge of leaving when Kurt realized he had lost his watch. "I had it on when I was timing you holding your breath," he said. "It must have slipped off. Wait here, Scotty, and don't get too near the edge."

"Where are you going, Dad?"

"I'm going to see if I can find it." He dived in.

The water was murky, and after several attempts he was about to call it quits when he caught a glint of something at the bottom and swam down to it.

It turned out to be a silver badge attached to a large bulk. Shocked, Kurt stared into the lifeless eyes of Sheriff Pyle DeWitt.

Chapter 19

After putting in a call to 911, Kurt immediately called Maddie at the bookstore. "Honey, is Beth still with you?"

"Yes, she's right here. Why do you ask?"

"Listen to me carefully and do exactly what I tell you. Close up immediately and…" He groped for a site where they'd be the safest until he could get to them. "Ah, go to the diner and stay there. Don't take a window booth or budge from the place until I can get there. And whatever you hear, don't either of you leave with any strangers, no matter *who* they claim to be. Don and Andy are the only two you can trust right now. Got that?"

"What's wrong, Kurt? Has something happened to Scotty?"

"No, Scotty's right here with me."

"Are Beth and I in some kind of danger?"

"Not if you stay in the diner. There's safety in numbers."

"Then what is it? What happened?"

"The sheriff's been murdered."

"Pyle? Murdered!"

"You and Beth keep it to yourselves. If people get panicky, it will only complicate the situation more. Now please, honey, get going. Call me when you're there, so I'll know you're safe."

He hung up and dialed Don Larson's cell phone. He told him what happened and where to find Maddie and Beth. Don said they'd head back at once.

Kurt had been staring at Scotty the whole time he'd been on the phone. The poor kid was still trembling. When he finished his call with Don, he went over, sat down beside him and hugged him to his side. He didn't know what to say to a nine-year-old child who was staring at the body of a man he knew and liked. Especially when that man had just been pulled out of the water with his hands cuffed behind his back.

He shifted his gaze to the approaching squad car. DeWitt's deputy, Brian Casey, stepped out of the vehicle. Now, with DeWitt dead, Casey was the only remaining police officer in the town. And the guy was clueless. He couldn't be a day over twenty, and looked more like he belonged in a Wisconsin Badger football uniform than the one he was wearing.

And it would take a damn sight more than a fast engine under the hood of a squad car and the Glock holstered on his hip to make him a police officer—especially up against international organ harvesting criminals. For there was no doubt in Kurt's mind that they were the ones who had knocked off the sheriff.

His cell phone beeped and it was Maddie to tell him she and Beth were safely entrenched in a booth in the diner. Now, as soon as Andy and Don got back, the women would be in safe hands.

The ambulance arrived followed by the Dane County sheriff's car. Kurt slipped an arm around Scotty's shoulder. There was no way he was going to leave his frightened and trembling son sitting alone. He figured as soon as they hauled the body away, he'd probably have to go in for questioning. If so, Scotty was going with him because he wasn't about to let his son out of his sight.

The Dane County Sheriff was handling the investigation, and by the time the questioning and filling out of reports were over and the police had departed, it had turned dark and they all were back at the house, gathered around the kitchen table.

"Why are you convinced the sheriff's murder is related to this Escobar situation?" Don asked, as soon as Kurt related the details of the discovery of DeWitt's body. "You told us this DeWitt was an SOB. Maybe someone with a grudge knocked him off."

"Well, Pyle did tell me in confidence that he was having Madison check out some of the evidence," Maddie said.

"It would be interesting to know if there was anyone else he might have confided in," Andy said. "We might be able to get some more details."

Kurt nodded. "It looked to me like he and Gertie Karpinski were pretty tight."

"I don't like to spread rumors, but they made no secret they were sleeping together," Beth said.

Maddie jumped to her feet. "That's right. Poor Gertie, the word must have spread by now. I should go over and comfort her."

Kurt didn't like the idea of her going out. "It's easier to protect you here."

"Protect me from whom, Kurt?" Maddie said. "You don't even know if Pyle's death has anything to do with us. Aren't you being paranoid?"

"When was the last time there was a murder in Vandergriff, Maddie?"

"Jim Temple shot his wife last year, and then killed himself."

"I'm not referring to domestic disputes. They happen all the time. I'm talking about mysterious murders. But I guess it wouldn't hurt to check out Gertie. Let's get going."

The streets were deserted. Even the lights of Rosie's Diner had been darkened for the evening. Word of Pyle DeWitt's murder had sped through the town quickly and the stunned residents, fearful that the killer still lurked within the town limits, chose to stay behind the locked doors of their homes.

Gertie still lived in Stoneville, and when she answered their knock, her eyes were reddened from weeping. Maddie stepped in and hugged her. "I'm so sorry, Gertie."

"It was kind of you to come. Most folks didn't know him like I did." She grinned at Kurt through her tears. "He kind of mellowed out the last few years."

Kurt got her point and nodded in understanding.

"Pyle liked you, Maddie. He often said what a fine lady you were."

"I liked him, too, Gertie. And he was always kind to Scotty."

"I guess we all were pains in the as—ah, rear end to him when we were in school," Kurt said.

Gertie smiled in remembrance. "Especially you and Joey."

He winked at her. "What did a couple of punk kids like us know?"

"Come on in and sit down," Gertie said. "Can I get you a cup of coffee or a drink?"

Maddie shook her head. "Thanks just the same, but we just had dinner. We dropped in to see how you were doing."

"Who do you think would want to murder him, Kurt?" Gertie asked suddenly.

"I'll be honest, Gertie. The thought crossed my mind a time or two when I was younger."

"You mean you think it could be someone from Stoneville?"

"I don't know anyone there now. It could be someone with an old grudge—or maybe a new one. He did make enemies, Gertie. Did he ever mention that anyone threatened him?"

"No. But like I said, Pyle mellowed the last few years."

"Gertie, did he say anything about the two men he locked up the other night."

"Only that he figured they weren't there to rob you, Kurt. He thought that maybe you were mixed up with gangsters or something like that. Pyle said he was going to have the Feds check them out thoroughly in case they showed up here again. He told me he sent them the fingerprints of the two."

"Hmm, interesting. I wonder if he found out anything."

"You aren't mixed up with any gang, are you, Kurt?"

"No, Gertie. I swear on my son's life."

"So when's the wedding?" she asked.

Disappointment was heavy in Maddie's voice when she spoke up. "Just this morning we decided to get married on Saturday. With Pyle's death, I don't think it would be in good taste to do so right now." She reached over and clasped Gertie's hand. "I know under the circumstances, this isn't the proper time to ask, but when we do set a date, I was hoping you would consider being my maid of honor."

Gertie gaped at her. "Are you serious? You're a fine lady, Maddie, and I'm...I'm the town tramp."

"That's nonsense, Gertie Karpinski. I won't listen to that kind of talk from you."

Gertie glanced at Kurt. "Explain it to her."

"I don't have a problem with it, Gertie."

"Then I'd be thrilled to be your maid of honor. I can't think of any two people I like more than the two of you. I only wish Pyle could be here to see it." She dabbed at her eyes. "You've got me crying again."

"Well, we'll leave you to your privacy," Kurt said. He kissed her on the cheek.

"I'll get back to you when we finalize the wedding plans, Gertie," Maddie said as Kurt pulled her out the door.

"Goodbye, Gertie, and keep your door locked," he called out.

Once they were in the car, Kurt kissed her lightly. "You know something, Maddie Bennett? You're a really nice person."

"Since when? I thought I was your nemesis."

"Asking Gertie to stand up at the wedding was a damn nice gesture on your part. I love you dearly, baby."

"I didn't do it out of sympathy, Kurt. I sincerely like Gertie. I always have."

"So have I. Good old 'Bare It and Share It' Karpinski. Seems a lifetime ago."

Maddie glanced at her bookstore as they drove past. "I could have sworn I saw someone in my store," she said.

"Are you sure?"

"Not really. I just caught a glimpse."

Kurt pulled the car into the far end of the mall's parking lot. "I'll check it out. Stay here and keep the doors locked."

"Not on your life, Bolen. I'm coming with you."

"I suppose it isn't any worse than leaving you here alone. Just be very quiet. If someone's in there, I prefer to not announce our arrival. And if I tell you to get out, you run like hell. Is that understood?"

"Yes," she said.

They stayed in the shadows and just as they neared the store two men came out the door. Maddie gasped loudly, and Kurt pulled her deeper into the shadows when one of the men turned his head and peered through the darkness. Kurt reached down to draw his gun and realized, too late, that he had taken it off when he took Scotty swimming.

When the two men started to approach them, Kurt knew this time they would shoot on sight. He grabbed Maddie's hand and pulled her into the narrow passage between the bookstore and the boarded-up theatre.

He saw that an exit door was ajar, most likely left open by kids who had broken into the theatre. Having worked there at one time, he knew the layout of the building well, so he pulled Maddie inside, then bolted the door again.

Now, without even moonlight to offer a ray of light, they were in pitch blackness. Even the normally lit Exit signs were no longer operative in the abandoned building.

He reached for his cell phone and was able to call Don Larson, inform him of where they were, the situation they were in and that he was unarmed. He asked him to notify Deputy Casey, and under no circumstances, leave Beth and Scotty alone.

As he hung up, he heard a loud crash and guessed the assailants had broken one of the front doors to get inside.

His eyes were fully adjusted now to the darkness, and he tried to think of a good place to hide Maddie until help arrived. If they went up to the balcony they could very well get trapped up there. Then he thought of a place to hide her.

Grabbing Maddie's hand, he headed down the aisle. The storeroom for supplies, and the dressing rooms for the employees to change into their uniforms were behind the screen. If neither of the two men ever worked in a theatre before, they might never guess the rooms were there.

In the hope of stalling them, he locked both doors to the dressing rooms and took the key with him, hoping they would waste time breaking into the rooms. Then he led her into the storeroom. "I'm going to lift you up on that loft. Then don't move or make a sound," he whispered. "There's no room up there for me, but I'll be nearby."

"I'm coming with you," she insisted.

"Maddie, this is no time for arguing."

"I know what you have in mind. You're going after them."

"Exactly, and I can do it better alone without having to worry about you." He clasped his hands together. "You're wasting time. Put your foot in here and I'll hoist you up."

As soon as Maddie was safely in place, Kurt slipped out of the room and approached the auditorium. He saw they had split up, and in tandem each one was in an aisle checking out the side and center sections row by row. Hugging the shadows, he moved toward the nearest aisle. If he could take one out and get the man's weapon, he'd have it made.

But he needed a temporary diversion. What he didn't need was Maddie suddenly appearing at his side. But it was too late to argue now with one of the men bearing down on them.

Checking his pockets, he came up with the door key to the dressing room. He flung the key toward the rear rows. It bounced off a wall and clanked against the cement floor under the seats.

The instant the man swung his attention in the direction of the sound, Kurt sprang at him. The assailant's weapon fell to the floor and a karate chop knocked him out. Shoving Maddie to the floor, Kurt groped in the dark for the man's weapon as the other criminal dashed along a row of seats toward them with an automatic UZI spraying a hail of bullets over their heads.

With bullets flying overhead, Kurt was forced to abandon the search for the weapon. They slithered under several rows of seats and crouched down behind them.

The gunman passed them in the dark, and stumbled against the prone body of his accomplice. Kurt used the momentary opportunity to get to his feet, but the culprit swung around as Kurt dived at him. The pair struggled for possession of the weapon in the close confine between the rows, when suddenly the man yelped in pain as Maddie sank her teeth into his arm.

Yanking the UZI out of the gunman's hand, Kurt shoved the barrel against the man's stomach.

"As Clint Eastwood would say, pal, 'Make my day'."

The fight was over as Don and Andy rushed through the door.

Once outside, Kurt grumbled, "Dammit, Don, didn't I tell you to stay with Beth and Scotty. There could be more of these bastards in town."

"They're perfectly safe in the backseat of the deputy's squad car," Don said.

Kurt leaned forward and peered through the window. A wide-eyed Scotty was cuddled against Beth. They climbed out of the car and Scotty rushed into the open arms of his mother.

The approach of another car caused them to take cover and draw their weapons. Then they all relaxed at the sight of the two men who climbed out. No matter how they tried not to appear so, all Federal agents looked alike to Kurt. Then the Dane County sheriff's squad car rolled into the parking lot, and within minutes the sheriff and the two federal agents left with the prisoners.

Maddie sighed in relief. "Thank God."

Kurt put his arms around her. "You realize, Maddie, you resorted to some violent action back there," he said as she remained in the comfort of his arms.

She looked up into his loving gaze. "I had to do something. He might have killed you."

"I appreciate the effort, honey. Those teeth of yours are a pretty lethal weapon."

She grinned sheepishly. "I've always heard that necessity is the mother of invention."

Kurt reached out and grasped Scotty's hand. "Come on, pal, let's get your mother home. I think the warrior has had enough battle for one day."

"You're never going to let me forget that I resorted to a violent act, are you?" Maddie said.

He slipped an arm around her shoulder. "You've got that right, sweetheart."

Chapter 20

Kurt hung up the phone the following morning and went back and joined the others at the breakfast table. "That was Mike Bishop. He said he talked to the FBI. The Feds told him our two friends have admitted to killing Pyle DeWitt, and are squealing out names and places in order to cop a plea bargain. Foreign governments are rounding up the accomplices all over the world even as we speak."

"Poor Fernando," Beth said sadly. "Such a brilliant man."

"I'm afraid it wasn't too brilliant of him to get mixed up with that band, no matter what his motive was. They murdered him when he threatened to confess to the authorities."

"Well, now that *that* horror is behind us," Maddie said, "Beth and I have been considering a wedding date. Pyle's funeral is scheduled for next Tuesday, so what about the following Saturday for the wedding?"

"Works for me," Kurt said. "I should have the house ready

by then, too. Did you two ladies decide what we'll still need to furnish it?"

Maddie bent over the back of his chair and kissed him on the cheek. "We've got that all worked out, Bolen. As for the wedding, what do you think of a backyard reception, and inviting anyone in town who's interested in attending? We can telephone an invitation to any relatives or friends out of town."

"I spoke to Pastor Jennings," Beth said. "He's willing to officiate, and if the weather doesn't cooperate he'll perform a private ceremony in church."

"And what happens about the guests if Mother Nature throws a monkey wrench into your plans?" Kurt asked.

"Rosie Callahan said she intends to close up the restaurant that day anyway, so we can move into there if we have to. So the main thing we have to decide is what to serve. Any suggestions?"

"Hamburgers and fries," Scotty shouted without hesitation.

Beth nodded. "You know, that might not be such a bad idea, considering we have no idea how many will be attending."

"But hamburgers and fries at a wedding?" Maddie pondered. "Has it ever been done before? It sounds more like a cookout."

"I think it sounds great," Kurt said. "Some people get married in bathing suits on a beach, some in Packers sports memorabilia at Lambeau Field. So what's wrong with a cookout?"

Maddie thought for another long moment. "Well, as long as we're not having a traditional wedding with me walking down the aisle in a gown and veil…" She shrugged. "What the heck! Why not hamburgers and fries?"

"Hooray!" Scotty shouted.

Kurt hugged her, and kissed her on the tip of her nose. "Have I ever told you you're the most incredible woman I've ever known, Miss Bennett?"

After the funeral of their long-time sheriff, the residents of Vandergriff were ready to kick up their heels at a wedding.

The bride looked gorgeous in an off-white gown, the maid of honor subdued in pale pink. The groom and his nine-year-old best man looked beyond handsome in their rented tuxedos and the four honorary best men looked so tall and unimpeachable that it made you feel pride in being an American.

After the nuptials were performed, and the toast to the bride and groom made by the best man holding up his glass of soda in the air, the real celebration began.

Rosie Callahan had closed the restaurant and her cook catered the fare for the day. The smell of grilled hamburgers and hot dogs blended with the fragrance of white roses and lavender to form an aroma of pure happiness and good times.

Maddie had the pleasure of meeting the men whom Kurt considered his family—the other members of the Dwarf Squad—along with their lovely wives Ann Bishop and Trish Cassidy.

Having no idea what to expect, she was pleased to discover how much fun and down to earth the two women were. And the unabashed adoration of them in the eyes of the men who married them was an inspiration to her.

She had already formed a deep fondness for Don and Andy, but her surprise was just as great after meeting Mike Bishop and Dave Cassidy. Considering the occupation all these men had chosen, she was surprised at the camaraderie between them all and how quickly they made certain to draw her into their circle of affection.

As the men stood together toasting their missing comrades, Mike Bishop broke the news to them that the squad was being disbanded.

"That makes my decision easier," Kurt said. "I was torn about whether or not to re-up."

"I'm going back into the navy. I figure they'll take me back into the SEALs," Andy said.

"I'm staying with the Bureau," Mike said. "I enjoy the think tank I'm in."

Dave Cassidy spoke up. "My pleasure is the stock market, so I'm looking forward to doing it full time for a change. What about you, Don?"

"I'm not sure what I'll do," he said. "My enlistment is up in another month, and now with the squad disbanding, I'm kind of leaning toward not re-upping same as Kurt."

"Well, we've been expecting this would happen for a long time," Mike said, "so at least it doesn't come as a shock to any of us. Nor does it mean the end to our friendships. We'll always be there for each other." He raised his glass. "To the squad."

"The squad," they all responded with raised glasses.

Later, as Kurt was dancing with Rosie Callahan, the mayor said, "I had a long talk with your ex-boss, Mike Bishop. He speaks very highly of you, Kurt."

"Yeah, Mike's a great guy."

"So you fellows were a special ops squad," she said.

"What?" Kurt exclaimed in feigned innocence. "Where did you get an idea like that?"

"Kurt, I didn't just fall off a turnip truck. Are you forgetting I got rich reading a man's body language." She chuckled lightly. "I have a proposition for you. The town needs a sheriff. Are you interested?"

"I hadn't thought about it."

"Well, the job's yours if you want it, Mr. Bolen. I won't have any problem convincing the Common Council. You can even hire your own deputy. Casey's decided to go back to school."

"If the pay is right, you've just hired yourself a sheriff," he said. "I might even have a deputy in mind if he's interested."

"Which member of the squad do you have in mind?"

"Madam Mayor, you're a laugh a minute. Have you met Don Larson?"

"Is he the one with the dreamy brown eyes?"

"You must be referring to my husband, Rosie," Maddie said, cutting in on them.

"Tomorrow. My office. Ten o'clock." The mayor smiled at Maddie. "You've got a good man here, honey." She winked at Kurt, and walked away.

"What was *that* all about?" Maddie asked, as Kurt glided her across the floor.

"What would you think if I became sheriff of Vandergriff? The squad's been disbanded. Mike just gave us the word."

"I'm sorry, Kurt. I know how much those men mean to you." Then she broke into a wide smile. "But I'd be lying if I tried to deny how happy I am that you won't be going back, Sheriff Bolen." She threw her arms around his neck and kissed him in the middle of the dance floor.

Not that he minded. After all, it's not improper for a newly married couple to kiss each other freely on their wedding day, which at the moment seemed a great idea to him, so they kissed again.

Later that evening, Kurt listened to the news as he waited for Maddie to do whatever women did in the bathroom on their wedding night. He turned to greet her when she finally came out of it, and stared in surprise. "Wow!" he finally managed to mumble. The transparent black peignoir she wore did little to conceal the chiffon bra and bikinis that clung to her breasts and hips.

She spun around with outstretched arms. "Like it?"

"Almost as much as what's almost in it." He found his legs and walked over to her. "Before I dare touch you, there's something I have to tell you. Should have told you before, so bear with me while I try to get through this.

"I love you, Maddie. And times like this remind me of how much I love you. Not just because I'm about to have sex with the most desirable and responsive woman I've ever known. The good sex is just an added bonus, honey.

"I love you because you're the most diversified woman I've ever known. You keep me guessing all the time because I never know what to expect from you. And that's the real miracle of what we have together. Looking up and seeing your smile, or walking into a room and smelling the scent of your perfume. I look in your eyes and I can see your love for me. And each time it happens, it's like a fix, it sends me soaring. I ask myself what have I ever done to deserve you? And sometimes when I look at Scotty I think, my God, that's my son, and you're his mother. And I can't believe it's happened to me.

"Honey, I know I don't deserve either one of you, but I swear I'll spend the rest of my living hours proving to you how much I love you."

Tears glistened in her eyes. "You don't have to prove it to me. I know you do. And I feel the same about you. Oh, Kurt, I've been such a fool. So obsessed with the fear of violence that I let it nearly destroy my chance for happiness. You've taught me that trust in the one I love is the greatest security I could ever hope for."

She sighed deeply. "And you've shown me by example that you men of action, who face violence daily, are not necessarily *violent* men. You're simply husbands and fathers, sons and sweethearts protecting your families as well as those of others. That's the lesson I learned from all of this."

"Good, because I've had just about all the talk I can stand—it's time for some action. I'll warn you that another lesson you should learn about men of action is that wearing an outfit like you've got on will only land you smack on your back."

He shoved the peignoir off her shoulders, picked her up and carried her to the bed.

"I suspected it would," she said boldly. With a sigh of expectation she slipped her arms around Kurt's neck and pulled

his head down to hers. "You see, lover, that's another quality
I've learned to admire about a man of action like you.

"You always cut right to the chase."

* * * * *

Harlequin is 60 years old,
and Harlequin Blaze is celebrating!
After all, a lot can happen in 60 years,
or 60 minutes…or 60 seconds!

Find out what's going down in
Blaze's heart-stopping new mini-series,
FROM 0 TO 60!
Getting from "Hello" to "How was it?"
can happen fast….

Here's a sneak peek of the first book,

A LONG, HARD RIDE
by Alison Kent

Available March 2009

"IS THAT FOR ME?" Trey asked.

Cardin Worth cocked her head to the side and considered how much better the day already seemed. "Good morning to you, too."

When she didn't hold out the second cup of coffee for him to take, he came closer. She sipped from her heavy white mug, hiding her grin and her giddy rush of nerves behind it.

But when he stopped in front of her, she made the mistake of lowering her gaze from his face to the exposed strip of his chest. It was either give him his cup of coffee or bury her nose against him and breathe in. She remembered so clearly how he smelled. How he tasted.

She gave him his coffee.

After taking a quick gulp, he smiled and said, "Good morning, Cardin. I hope the floor wasn't too hard for you."

The hardness of the floor hadn't been the problem. She shook her head. "Are you kidding? I slept like a baby, swaddled in my sleeping bag."

"In my sleeping bag, you mean."

If he wanted to get technical, yeah. "Thanks for the loaner. It made sleeping on the floor almost bearable." As had the warmth of his spooned body, she thought, then quickly changed the subject. "I saw you have a loaf of bread and some eggs. Would you like me to cook breakfast?"

He lowered his coffee mug slowly, his gaze as warm as the sun on her shoulders, as the ceramic heating her hands. "I didn't bring you out here to wait on me."

"You didn't bring me out here at all. I volunteered to come."

"To help me get ready for the race. Not to serve me."

"It's just breakfast, Trey. And coffee." Even if last night it had been more. Even if the way he was looking at her made her want to climb back into that sleeping bag. "I work much better when my stomach's not growling. I thought it might be the same for you."

"It is, but I'll cook. You made the coffee."

"That's because I can't work at all without caffeine."

"If I'd known that, I would've put on a pot as soon I got up."

"What time *did* you get up?" Judging by the sun's position, she swore it couldn't be any later than seven now. And, yeah, they'd agreed to start working at six.

"Maybe four?" he guessed, giving her a lazy smile.

"But it was almost two…" She let the sentence dangle, finishing the thought privately. She was quite sure he knew exactly what time they'd finally fallen asleep after he'd made love to her.

The question facing her now was where did this relationship—if you could even call it *that*—go from here?

* * * * *

Cardin and Trey are about to find out that
great sex is only the beginning....
Don't miss the fireworks!
Get ready for

A LONG, HARD RIDE
by Alison Kent

Available March 2009,
wherever Blaze books are sold.

CELEBRATE
60 YEARS
OF PURE READING PLEASURE
WITH HARLEQUIN®!

We'll be spotlighting a different series
every month throughout 2009
to celebrate our 60th anniversary.

Look for Harlequin® Blaze™ in March!

*After all, a lot can happen in 60 years,
or 60 minutes...or 60 seconds!*

Find out what's going down in Blaze's
heart-stopping new miniseries *0-60!*
Getting from "Hello" to "How was it?"
can happen fast....

Look for the brand-new 0-60 miniseries in March 2009!

www.eHarlequin.com   HBRIDE09

REQUEST YOUR FREE BOOKS!

2 FREE NOVELS PLUS 2 FREE GIFTS!

Silhouette® Romantic

SUSPENSE

Sparked by Danger, Fueled by Passion!

YES! Please send me 2 FREE Silhouette® Romantic Suspense novels and my 2 FREE gifts (gifts are worth about $10). After receiving them, if I don't wish to receive any more books, I can return the shipping statement marked "cancel." If I don't cancel, I will receive 4 brand-new novels every month and be billed just $4.24 per book in the U.S. or $4.99 per book in Canada, plus 25¢ shipping and handling per book plus applicable taxes, if any*. That's a savings of at least 15% off the cover price! I understand that accepting the 2 free books and gifts places me under no obligation to buy anything. I can always return a shipment and cancel at any time. Even if I never buy another book from Silhouette, the two free books and gifts are mine to keep forever.

240 SDN EEX6 340 SDN EEYJ

Name _____ (PLEASE PRINT) _____

Address _____ Apt. # _____

City _____ State/Prov. _____ Zip/Postal Code _____

Signature (if under 18, a parent or guardian must sign)

Mail to the Silhouette Reader Service:
IN U.S.A.: P.O. Box 1867, Buffalo, NY 14240-1867
IN CANADA: P.O. Box 609, Fort Erie, Ontario L2A 5X3

Not valid to current subscribers of Silhouette Romantic Suspense books.

Want to try two free books from another line?
Call 1-800-873-8635 or visit www.morefreebooks.com.

* Terms and prices subject to change without notice. N.Y. residents add applicable sales tax. Canadian residents will be charged applicable provincial taxes and GST. Offer not valid in Quebec. This offer is limited to one order per household. All orders subject to approval. Credit or debit balances in a customer's account(s) may be offset by any other outstanding balance owed by or to the customer. Please allow 4 to 6 weeks for delivery. Offer available while quantities last.

Your Privacy: Silhouette is committed to protecting your privacy. Our Privacy Policy is available online at www.eHarlequin.com or upon request from the Reader Service. From time to time we make our lists of customers available to reputable third parties who may have a product or service of interest to you. If you would prefer we not share your name and address, please check here. ☐

HARLEQUIN® *Romance*®

This February the Harlequin® Romance series
will feature six Diamond Brides stories featuring
diamond proposals and gorgeous grooms.

Share your dream wedding proposal and you could WIN!

The most romantic entry will win a diamond
necklace and will inspire a proposal in one of
our upcoming Diamond Grooms books in 2010.

In 100 words or less, tell us the most romantic
way that you dream of being proposed to.

For more information, and to enter
the Diamond Brides Proposal contest, please visit
www.DiamondBridesProposal.com

Or mail your entry to us at:

IN THE U.S.: 3010 Walden Ave., P.O. Box 9069, Buffalo, NY 14269-9069
IN CANADA: 225 Duncan Mill Road, Don Mills, ON M3B 3K9

Silhouette®
Romantic
SUSPENSE

COMING NEXT MONTH

Available February 24, 2009

#1551 THE RANCHER BODYGUARD—Carla Cassidy
Wild West Bodyguards
Grace Covington's stepfather has been murdered, her teenage sister the only suspect. Convinced of her sister's innocence, Grace turns to her ex-boyfriend, attorney Charlie Black, to help her find the truth. Although she's determined not to forgive his betrayal, the sexual tension instantly returns as their investigation leads them into danger…and back into each other's arms.

#1552 CLAIMED BY THE SECRET AGENT—Lyn Stone
Special Ops
COMPASS agent Grant Tyndal was supposed to be on a mission to rescue a kidnapping victim, but Marie Beauclair doesn't need rescuing. An undercover CIA operative, she's perfectly able to save herself. As they work together to catch the kidnapper, will the high-intensity situations turn their high-voltage passion into something more?

#1553 SAFE BY HIS SIDE—Linda Conrad
The Safekeepers
When someone begins stalking a child star, Ethan Ryan is the perfect man to be her bodyguard. But the child's guardian, Blythe Cooper, wants nothing to do with him. As the stalker closes in, sparks fly between Ethan and Blythe, and they soon find their lives—and their hearts—at risk.

#1554 SUSPECT LOVER—Stephanie Doyle
They both wanted a family, so Caroline Sommerville and Dominic Santos agreed to a marriage of convenience. Neither expected love—until it happened. But when Dominic's business partner is murdered, he's the prime suspect and goes on the run. Can Caroline trust this man who lied about his past—the man she now calls her husband?